The Queen's Play

The Queen's Play

Aashish Kaul

Winchester, UK
Washington, USA

First published by Roundfire Books, 2015
Roundfire Books is an imprint of John Hunt Publishing Ltd., Laurel House, Station Approach,
Alresford, Hants, SO24 9JH, UK
office1@jhpbooks.net
www.johnhuntpublishing.com
www.roundfire-books.com

For distributor details and how to order please visit the 'Ordering' section on our website.

Text copyright: Aashish Kaul 2014

ISBN: 978 1 78279 861 3
Library of Congress Control Number: 2014949216

A CIP catalogue record for this book is available from the British Library.

Design: Stuart Davies

Printed and bound by CPI Group (UK) Ltd, Croydon, CR0 4YY

We operate a distinctive and ethical publishing philosophy in all
areas of our business, from our global network of authors to
production and worldwide distribution.

AUTHOR'S NOTE

Among many things that this book is, that every book is, it is a book about chess. Not chess as we know it, but chess as was known at the time in which this story is based. A time of prehistory, a time of myth. Or in a sense, it is the trajectory of the game across centuries and continents, tempered and improved upon piecemeal by countless minds and actors, circumstances, traditions, topographies, subsumed here for my purposes in the space of a single consciousness, that of queen Mandodari, consort of Ravana, the demon king of Lanka, familiar to the reader of the Indian epic *Ramayana*, and perhaps also to one who has merely heard of it. In writing *The Queen's Play*, therefore, I have taken the liberty to assume on the part of the reader a working knowledge of the *Ramayana*, but I see no reason why one wholly unaware of the plot might not end up further along the path of discovery.

In the legends of the game's origin, lost in antiquity, there are many beginnings, many speculations, many lands of birth. One of which, and as Duncan Forbes shows in his masterly *The History of Chess*, first published in London in 1860, the most plausible, is that it was invented in India before recorded time, and was understood and played by the people of the subcontinent from the foothills of the Himalaya up in the extreme north through the entire breadth of the Gangetic plains to the very tip of the southern peninsula. Why, then, could it not have been invented, as the legend tells, by Mandodari herself to amuse Ravana with an image of war, while his metropolis was besieged by Rama, in the second age of the world?

Myth being the mother of art, of literature, it is both natural and befitting that this should serve as the basis of a novel which partakes directly of this grand and familiar setting, while at the same time charting a unique path of its own, even if now and then the narrative returns to touch or pierce through the epic tale, following its own logic and design, positing its own questions and speculating upon their answers. Isn't that, after all, one of the more significant functions of myth?

Accounts and ideas that branch out from the margins of history, lie concealed in the debris of so much myth and religion, here as elsewhere cut from the same cloth, may offer us moderns the possibility to relate tales that reveal our own face, our own predicament, to ourselves. The cursory mention this early prototype of chess finds, among other ancient texts of India, in the *Ramayana* lore, takes us as far back as the fifth century BCE, if not earlier. While not much is mentioned by way of explication, evidence, or conjecture as to its origins, the link between the game and the themes of the epic poem offer several interesting parallels and imaginative openings. To me, for instance, this brief reference, frozen in the byways of myth, is both compelling and poignant. For although in the old format of the game there was no piece referred to as the *Queen*, why, I asked myself, if a queen created the game, could I not write her into it? In this departure lies the novel's genesis. For how the first prototype came to be is far less interesting than its evolution into modern chess. Not least because at the centre of this long journey is a queen (first entering and then growing from strength to strength to become the most powerful piece on the board) inventing a game which closely parallels the epic battle taking place not far from the royal palace, a battle which she is not permitted to join, a battle where she will lose her king. Employing the game's development as a narrative strategy in a time period immeasurably remote from our own, allows one the requisite method and space to probe once more the perennial questions of literature – of desire and despair, the ephemerality of triumph and the weight of failure, the swelling of pride and the contraction of frustration, the sweep of providence and the jabs of free will – from which even gods are not spared.

Some understanding of the old game might be helpful, indeed valuable, to the reader. *Chaturanga* (literally, 'four-parts' or 'quadripartite'), Forbes tells us, originally represented an image of ancient Hindu warfare, applied to an army composed, in certain proportions, of four distinct species of forces under the command of a king. These were elephants, horses, ships (or chariots), and infantry, their present day chess equivalents being rooks, knights, bishops, and pawns, respectively.

The pieces in *Chaturanga* moved substantially in the same manner as in chess, however their scope was limited. The pawn, as is the case even today in the Indian version of chess, moved only one square at the beginning, whereas the bishop moved diagonally to any third square. Rooks, knights, and kings moved just as they do now. And yet all moved only at the whim of the dice. If the throw was *five*, the king or one of the pawns had to be moved; if *four*, the rook; if *three*, the knight, and if *two*, it was the bishop's turn. Bishops and pawns mutually captured each other, but were not allowed to capture a superior piece, while a king, rook, or knight could take any piece, but was immune from capture by any other except an adversary's king, rook, or knight. Then as now, the board consisted of sixty-four squares, though not chequered at first, and the game had four instead of two players, the intent of each player being to capture the enemy kings. From four players and four armies to two; from dice to no dice; from play of fate to that of the will. From absence to the advent of the *Queen*. This is the slow arc of the game's evolution enmeshed in the larger story.

Chess, among so many things, is a sublime symbol of the baroque in literature, where, to think of Roland Barthes, the extent is not additive but multiplicative. Gradually, the theme of every book finds its own especial form. The great surgeons of narrative, from Gérard de Nerval to William Faulkner to Julio Cortázar, to say nothing of James Joyce, went much further with their material, but rarely does the subject, the content, comes to one so clearly suited for its form. For while the game *per se* does not figure too predominantly in the novel, it inspires both the content of the story and its making. So where outwardly in the novel, a chapter may have nothing to do with chess, the narration itself can at times appear to move like a bishop or a knight on the board.

Chess, by its very nature, employs and develops continual forkings in time and space, thereby helping to sustain a great variety of elements, shapes, and tones, intense thinking followed by swift manoeuvres where the player and the pieces quite literally become one, quest, hope, lament, but, most importantly, stasis and motion, the supreme drivers of life and, therefore, of literature.

The world is like the impression left by the telling of a tale.
Yoga Vāsiṣṭha

God moves the player, he in turn the piece.
But what god beyond God begins the round
of dust and time and sleep and agonies?
Jorge Luis Borges

I

THE NEED for tales they say arose when the fetters came stuck round our ankles with a clank of inevitability, when our wings were torn slowly by the earth's fierce pull, when even the skill of climbing trees or perching on a branch was forgotten. And yet the longing remained. For the sky, for every path that wound upward and was lost in space, for luminous summits melting in whiffs of cloud. It was then that the desire was born, to name the stars and see in them something of our prehistory, the desire to read the scrawl in the depths of the night, to form our first myths, relate stories of our hidden, unknown beginnings.

Climbing up the old cedar near the mountain top, the god Anjaneya at last settled on a high branch, light like a bird but for the heaviness in his heart. Try as he might he could not gather its cause, for in this vast river of remembrance it was as hopeless to recall something as it was to forget anything. Something made him sneeze, and at this the starlings hiding in the tree flew like sparks in every direction, making such a racket that parrots, squirrels, and black-faced silver apes were obliged to join in, a few jackals watched from afar, sighing in chorus just once.

With the sight that he possessed, he could have easily seen the lake beyond the rim of the hills, circumscribed in turn by a second chain of hills, its water green-black from reflecting the trees all around, and beyond that the plains stirred to life by the rivers born of these very mountains, and beyond that the wastelands to the west, and beyond that the forests of the central and southern provinces, abounding in time-traps and dangers and beasts and conjurers, but also in fruits and berries and resting groves and hermitages, and beyond that the tip of the southern peninsula, and even far beyond into the sea, into the city of gold where the demon king had once lived, how many ages ago, now less than a ball of dust rolling in nothingness.

But such is the way of sadness, increasing the cohesion, making us fall into ourselves, that he did not wish to remember any of this. So his sight, following his intention, became merely that of a child, sharp but mortal. A child's vision in a child's form. He saw thus only his mud hut in the fold of the wooded valley, and the mist slowly lifting, no, moving westward at a push from the light which was fast spreading across the mountains in the east.

He had risen early, it was still night. Outside, a heavy mist enveloped the hut. In its slow swirl he began to perceive outlines of faces, friends and teachers and demons and saints, long lost in the pit of time, faces that were slowly absorbed back into the fog where now appeared in their place words from the scriptures, all merging to form the one word, no, the sound, for the word was nothing but the sound, the sound that was also the light, light that was also matter.

He retreated into the hut, thinking of Rudra, the blue-throated ascetic, whose incarnation on earth he was believed to be. Rudra, chief aspect of the Creator Spirit, remote, turned into himself, dwelling on inaccessible heights. What did *he* propose for him? The two great wars were behind him, his work, so to speak, long finished. Was he to wait until all the four stages of the world had come to an end, to wait stoically for the great rains that would temporarily suspend time, before the start of another aeon? And for that to happen . . . this was still the third stage, and the fourth again was to be of many many millennia. Aeon upon aeon, a thousand times, and all but a day turned in the life of the Maker. With each such day the universe began anew, with each such night it contracted into him, remaining a mere potentiality. Day after Day creation was made, unmade, and remade, until the Creator too, bent and spent, passed into the void to make way for yet another demiurge and his creativity. This was the indubitable wisdom of the seers, countless consecutive creators painting the continuously uncoiling canvas of infinity. There was no moral, no judgment, no deliverance in this. To act with will in will-lessness for a moment, for all moments, was the only way.

When he next stirred, he could not say whether it had been a few hours, a day, a month, or a year. It was all the same, for who was here beside him to object out of boredom? Outside it was light. Already a child as he stepped out of the hut, he was now hurriedly climbing the adjoining hill. Soon he was on the slope of the mountain that towered over the surroundings, behind which, in the distance, were visible those brown peaks smeared with snow.

Sitting weightless, dangling his legs, he took stock of the distance he had covered. He stretched his arm, and a mango, a delicious yellow and red in colour, appeared in the hollow of his palm. He bit into the mango, spat the skin, and began to suck, pressing it gently with both his thumbs and index fingers. Out of nowhere a baby monkey landed on the branch, which shook under its weight, forcing the child to glance sideways, to see it watch him with watery eyes. He turned away and made as if to suck again, but then threw the mango toward the little one, that leapt in the air to catch the half-eaten fruit, fell through the green cover, and was seen no more.

There now appeared in the child's hand a peach, which he promptly put into his mouth. Awhile he sat thus, but then, on a whim, let himself fall from the branch, hanging upside down, like those sages hanging from trees for months and years, dead to the world, dust crusting their taut, reptilian skins, ash caking in streaks across their face, green snakes crawling in their entangled hair, staring into unknown dimensions with unblinking fiery eyes. Blood began to rush to his head from every part of his body, and his sight seemed to recede as all the world's shadows poured into his eyes, darkening them, from red to maroon to slate-grey to coal-black, calling forth the night.

II

THE QUEEN is in a temper. She has summoned her help, who is now approaching the royal chambers at the edge of the gold palace with a shuffle in her step. In a moment she will enter those rooms where countless little flames are quivering in the breeze, marking the walls with dark arabesques. But amid this net of light and shadow, the queen will not be seen. For the queen is out in the balcony, standing deep in its curve and watching the darkness which is the sea.

A glance into these calm depths, and you will never be yourself again. The lady-in-waiting knew this all too well, so the moment the queen turned to look at her, she made as if to bow. Better it was to avoid the mercurial eyes resting on her, not their usual ash-green tonight, but of a black that bespoke a despair which comes only after you have quelled extreme rage inside you. Clearly the queen was beside herself, floating above the void she returned to often these days. Prepare the bath, she ordered, and the help retreated to see to the task. Behind, the sea had turned choppy, and a moon of burnt crimson was lifting from its waves.

A scent of myrrh and jasmine filled the air. Pale green water poured out from horse and lion heads into the round pool, smooth like the inside of an egg. She stepped into the pool parting the petals and quickly slipped to its bottom. Water, always water, could give the oblivion she so desired at such moments. One by one thoughts released her from their hold, and a sky vacant and pale green, as if a star had burst or some flower had blossomed, filled her vision.

Then in the distance a dark spot took shape, moving toward her, first slowly and in time urgently, but unable to go much further lost flight and fell straight into her cupped hands. There it lay helplessly beating its wings, suffocating from thirst and fatigue. The queen felt the bird's agony like a shooting pain numbing her heart and spreading outward. She rose suddenly to the surface, catching her breath and laughing softly. Colour rose in her face. Colour, too, crept back in her eyes, gently pushing the black in whose shade the palest of green was beginning to emerge.

Do sounds ever die? The queen's voice is down to a whisper as she dabs herself behind the wood-filigree partition. Surely they outlive the moments of their birth, like these sounds that grow sharper with each clash of the scimitars. And here she is, alert and perspiring, moving with agility to avoid the weapon that is many weapons at once, that covets her flesh. The sun is getting stronger and the wind has fallen. From each corner of the yard elephants watch the contest. These are the king's favourite beasts, having led him to victory in many a battle. Yet this is no battle, regardless of the dust that fills the air or the smell of the hunt that circles the combatants.

A draught from the sea sweeps past the palace courtyard, and the queen moves inside it, takes the king by surprise.

The king lets his weapon fall. It meets the ground with barely a sound, as befitting a lost ambition, unnecessary and forgettable. Although her heart has not yet settled in her breast, the thrill of the game, the delight of success, is leaving her. Something salty stings her tongue. Is it her sweat, or is it the taste of the sea the current has left there? Drops have trickled down her brow and spoilt the kohl that rings her eyes. Drops have collected on her back and hips, making the dress stick to her figure.

Scimitars clashing under the morning sun. These sounds will never die. Now and then they will please and upset me by turn. I will continue to be on this island until the sea is inside me, while he annexes one princedom upon another. She will petition him no more. That was her resolve this noon when the king departed to crush an uprising in the Blue Mountains. She was again refused permission to accompany him. Instead the prince of the serpent clan, a protectorate on the southern edge of the continent across the sea, was to be his ally.

Now she stands fighting the last bit of despair and thinking of the king relieving his fatigue of battle in the impassioned embraces of foreign women. And she can almost feel his eyes on the youngest of them, beneath whom having first slid a feather cushion with one hand, he has, with the other, bunched her hair so as to open with the slightest of tugs, the successive depths of her neck and chest, which are heaving frantically, leaving somewhere in the extremity of her toes a hint of pain. Meanwhile, from the four corners of the tent, others take in the suppressed moans of this young initiate with a mixed look of jealousy and lasciviousness, twitching at their colourful quilts, and waiting to claw and pinch her at the slightest opportunity. The daily petty rivalries of the harem.

The queen left the room and walked over to the balcony. The moon shone, white and serene, high up in the dark dome, and a soft, sinister wind rose up from the sea. Flashes from time to time brightened the sky's edges. Were these the fiery dragons, the island's guardian spirits, out on patrol? Dragons or comets, the queen doesn't give them another look. She is elsewhere, perhaps nowhere at all.

III

NIGHT HAS fallen from the sky. It is pale and vacant and airless. A shadow moves in it slowly, perhaps with difficulty, having journeyed this far only to dip its beak in the river, which is calm now that the lands are flatter and the hills round and low. Unable to ride the wind any more, the river in its eyes, the fall happens quickly when the overwhelming weariness has ejected the last remaining strength, and the milk-white water is the bird's grave.

The vision shook the child. Raising his tongue, he let the stone of the peach slip past his lips, and suddenly felt free of a burden. Light had returned to his eyes, but he knew that the comfort of mortality, of belonging only to *this* time, was leaving them.

The child rose to the tree's crown as before. At his feet and far beyond, the mountains opened into a valley where tall conifers stood in never ending ranks, like soldiers holding their breath before the bugle-horn of battle.

And then the horn sounded. A collective sigh escaped from the ranks that spread like a wave and was carried away on the updraught. For the moment, a weariness came over the army, a moment which returns at the start of battle each day to confound every soldier, a moment that must be wrestled with and overcome, a moment in which the uselessness of his enterprise fills every soldier with despair, a despair, nonetheless, to be tamed swiftly into a resolve. To draw the enemy's blood and to fulfil one's duty to the king, one's debt to the gods, regardless of the fact that such duties and debts had been written in the stars long ago and he who moved

III

so close to earth was essentially powerless to shake their yoke from his flesh, so that to return home alive and be joined once more to his woman was reward enough.

Yet many will not fulfil this resolve, certainly not that noble warrior who stands in the second row set to meet the adversary, head firm and high, muscles flexed, the left hand gripping the weapon lightly, breathing into the charnel void that awaits him. Like so many others, he will go down under the blows of the enemy, cloven by its large axe-blades that glitter in the morning sun, ready to strike.

Anjaneya ran at the head of the brigade straight into the enemy formation. From a distance the prince-in-exile observed the scene phlegmatically, standing in his three-horse chariot, having not yet lifted his bow. Then the enemy forces closed around the first batch of his army, and, for a moment, the sea's fluid silence covered everything.

A clap of thunder made the prince look up. But the sound had not come from above. The sky was light and clear though he could see the gods keenly watching the scene with their heads between their legs. It was the first roar of the hovering doom. The spear skidding against the shield, the sword meeting the axe, the ribcage breaking beneath the skin, the kick in the groin, the blood on the ground, the contact of a club driving the cone of a soldier's helmet down into his very skull to settle in the space between the eyes, which were already bidding farewell to the elements, Earth, Water, Wind, Fire were for him coalescing into a thin coolness that for another was still the ether where the visible was made invisible, where the dreamer dreamt his life again and again, where, just this moment, the dead soldier was sinking into the earth, and where dust freely swirled in the rising heat past the swinging limbs, shouts, curses, sweat, and blood.

High above, in the sky that was beginning to be dotted by vultures, the ominous sounds from the field did not reach. And without these sounds where was the spectacle of battle? What more could this be than a game opening between two rival forces facing each other, played on a field of alternating dark and light spaces, not fixed but shifting, little more than a motif of trembling shadows, wresting from light at one place what they returned at another, moving yet unmoving. Not so different was this then from the chequered board of smooth ebony and maple woods where, with a faint scent of pine needles on the air and the calls of the peacocks breaking into a sudden dance, with water from the fountains softly plashing in glowing pools of colour, the dark foot soldier had taken its first slight step, pushed ever so gently from behind by a pale slim hand.

By noon the sea's rhythm itself had permeated the battle. Each hour, the round of fatalities grew and fell with the periodic revival and ebbing away of the strength of its warriors. The initial rush of energy had departed the thick and fast of war, for the soldiers on either side, now that the first sudden terror of losing their lives had somewhat abated, had taken a more reasonable view of the situation and had settled on a longer span of combat, stretching over days, maybe months. Thus, both sides had adopted a defensive strategy, and deaths occurred more from oversight or a failure of strength than sustained initiative. Incredible as it seemed, hope had taken root even here, indeed it was thriving in every soldier's breast, who would not have put past him the mugs of stout and tales round the campfire, a generous fare, and six hours of deep, unbroken sleep on the other side of sundown. But between sundown and the first drink there yet remained the cruel, backbreaking task of clearing the ground for the next day, moving away and cremating the dead, lighting vast funeral pyres all along the coastline, wood crackling, bones bursting from heat, blue ashes.

When the sun sank into the waves, Anjaneya was opening his arm for a swing at his opponent, but just then the moan of the conch shells signalled a close of the day's battle, and his hand slowed in mid air, but in the infinitesimal space born outside time, a space in which forms dissolve into one another, where the club touched the chest the bones bayoneted the heart, the victim falling to the ground as the first banners heralding the night's rest were going up.

At last a bone-white moon rose slowly over the trees, where the forest suddenly opened onto the vast beach, the very theatre of this *danse macabre*. Here and there embers glowed in dying campfires about which bodies lay huddled together for warmth, traversing a darkness deeper than night, a spectacular stillness born of drink, food, and an excruciating fatigue. Near the grove where he had retired with his two aides, the fire was still burning. Moonshine was returning valour to their faces, causing glints in the lesions over them. Somewhere someone was crying from toothache, one misery gaining ground on another. Polishing the round fruit on his tunic till it shone red and golden, catching the fire in its skin, he sat unwashed in the shadow of a fig tree, black with grime, beard matted, hair clotted with blood, the metal guard still fastened to the left leg. The fruit was slowly transmitting its fire to his eyes, in their dark depths a tiny flame was now blazing. From the far side of the world came a slow sound of a hollowed-out antelope horn being played.

IV

WHEN THE final betrayal had taken place, when one act of honour had been traded for a second, when the death-dealing arrow had been delivered to the enemy by the king's own brother, when the iron tip had pierced the king's navel at twilight, when the lord of three worlds lay writhing on the ground, spattering the sap of his hard-won immortality everywhere, when our confused, weary troops had been eventually routed, the war was at last over. Then I climbed down the back of my wound-ridden elephant into an immense lake of silence. A curiously fluid world from before the birth of sound. For days, I carried this emptiness in me, and the emptiness carried me in it.

Soon we had a king. He who was next of kin to the deceased ruler, he who having been wrongly banished for speaking his mind, hitting straight at the king's pride, had walked over to the exiled prince and offered his confidences, an act some claimed was righteous, others, no less rightly, sanctimonious, was deemed fit for the throne by the victors.

I was, of course, at the court, amid the oboes, cymbals, and kettledrums sneaking behind the unceasing chants and invocations of the priests, to pay my obeisance to our king upon his crowning. Seeing everything, hearing nothing, not even my own voice. And yet by some miracle was heard and understood by all.

Now that peace was upon us, the work of rebuilding from the debris of battle commenced in full swing. What did I care for it? To the one born in the streets, this business of building and wrecking and building again was the very essence of living. Indeed, it seemed, if one took a true stock of our miserable condition, that we could fight and kill simply to relieve the tedium of days or to stroke our own, when not the sovereign's, foolish, insatiate pride at the first opportunity. If one was not combatting an enemy on the battle-field, one was trying to get killed in drunken brawls, knife-fights, and duels in the street. And what men could not finish among them, the vagaries of fate did. After all death from syphilis or cracking your skull in the wash was not inconceivable, while an innocuous remark slipped over drinks could estrange a loved one forever. Just when you were looking the other way, a scaffold was being readied for you. Alas, who could tell where you would end up for letting your gaze wander a moment? And so it took you not long to see that each peaceful day was a carrier of untold silent cruelties, that every honourable motive girdled countless devious and dishonest deeds, that the war continued beyond all wars, a war against an invisible foe, from whom you had to snatch each good lungful of air, each firm foot of earth, for as long as you lived.

Not that I had wanted any of this. As a child, I was even a little yielding. But then you are here to learn, and how fast you learn scavenging in the street. There, in the midst of indifference and wretchedness, iniquity comes at you with long strides, cruelty grows as easily as hunger, and before you know your arms are swinging freely, the weapon having long since settled in the groove of your small fist. Yet, when all was said and done, my life hadn't been much worse than another. Think of the orphan who had once been a page at eleven and a foot soldier at fifteen, who had perchance saved the king's life in a skirmish, where could he not go from there, what effort would he spare to put some distance between himself and his wretched past?

Thankfully, over the years, I had risen so high at court under the gaze of the deceased king that I could choose to delegate all duties until an exceptional event caused me to intervene. But with the long-drawn-out battle behind us, what was really left to demand my attention? With the king dead, I, for once, was free of the obligation I had long felt toward him and the empire. Time had come for the one lasting thing my riches could procure, something that would remain when all else had been turned to dust in its smithy, something that gave its fullness to days, years, epochs, and yet remained full, something that could show me my true face, help me find and love the self which got lost long ago in the very process of securing its extreme vulnerability, this deep, silent river of time which gently carried me, free of desire or destination, neither leaving nor arriving.

For this quiet period, I was thankful. Because a sudden illness had taken hold of my body and mind. Fatigue not only of the long war, but of the very effort of breathing was collecting in my blood, moving through my arteries, acquiring mass, growing like a massive rock bent on bursting my vessels and tearing open my flesh. A prolonged rest was prescribed by the medicine men who were unable to form a specific diagnosis. A warm brew with some or other medicinal herb and a pinch of turmeric and saffron was handed to me twice a day to heal injuries. Thus, amid a flurry of servants, I lazed about, sucked lightly scented smoke through the long stem of my water pipe, thought, and waited.

During the day, sparrows the size of a child's fist with indigo and blue patterned crowns and sword-like erect tails, flitted in the hedgerows enclosing the yard, splashing colour everywhere, and in the evening, before the pine torches had pushed the darkness further into itself, a martin returning to a nearby tree would sometimes brush its open wing against my cheek. While I took my ease in the long chair, shimmering in the heat like a mirage, the sparrows hopped in circles, or took two hesitant jumps forward and one backward, until suddenly one was sitting on my chest, for it I too was the earth and the firmament, part of the familiar forms it knew instinctively, and my phantom fingers were caressing its crown, gentle like the fingers forming an urn on the wheel, a gesture the bird appeared to be enjoying, slowly sinking into a torpor in front of my lowered eyes, and lightly pressing on my chest a benediction for the past, a hot, bloody, nightmarish past, for which the bird and the world which it belonged to, which we both belonged to, cared nothing in the least. It seemed I had been awaiting this moment all my life, but now that it was upon me, I could do little else than shed tears of relief. Then the bird let out a chirp and, after days of being submerged, my head came above water, and how clearly I heard the river of smoke making its bubbling passage far off through the clay pot of my pipe.

News then came that my elephant was dying. How loyal he had been to me in the war, taking on himself wounds from so many weapons, any of which would have sent me to my end, here throwing a cavalier off the horse with a twitch of his tail, there toppling an enemy chariot with his swaying trunk, all this at just the slightest twists from my big toe at certain points in his back, which worked like a code between us. When we waited at the edge of the ranks or up close for a sign from the king, the great shudder of war ended at his padded feet, when we entered the fray, a path opened by itself in the throng ahead of us, and never had we to cut diagonally through a warring faction, at its weakest point, like a charioteer, nor did we have to jump inevitably sideways after two straight bold leaps like a cavalryman who somehow always found himself deep in the tumult of a packed group of soldiers.

I hurried to the stables, and there he was, shrunken to half his size between ears that looked ever more gigantic, in part due to the absence of the gold-threaded headgear and the delicately carved conical armour on the tusks, stock still in shade of the thatched roof, preserving the last of his strength. In those amber eyes there was no hint of recognition as I came close and offered him a cane to chew, but when I hugged the leg near me, his trunk calmly crept over my back. He took the cane distractedly into his half-open mouth, standing in the odour of long festering wounds, which four stable boys worked through day and night to keep free of flies by burning camphor and other unguents. Behind, at the edge of the wall where it touched the roof, the wood had rotted and given way to an irregular patch of sky. Somewhere between this black rotten wood and that blue floating oblivion lay the answer to the puzzle of our lives.

I returned having known I had seen the last of him. At night, an aide sent to my chamber a girl to distract me. And though my mind was far away, I let her undress me, even as my own hands worked through her lace gown on which tiny rhinoceroses were locking horns. I should have continued to move deeper into the vortex of desire, sinking, no, drinking in the secretions, and leaving far behind a body thick with sorrow, had I not by chance glanced into her eyes. The same unawareness of truth, the same slow trembling, the same inexplicable fragment of fear for every passing moment, for that which was to follow. All at once, there welled up in me some great unknown love for the girl, who had in that moment ceased to be another. And in a flash, she saw it too. Now we were only two children clinging to each other in the dark. I pulled her to my bare chest, and began to rock gently waist upward, stroking her from head to bottom, cocooned in the warmth of the two conjoined skins.

In the morning, I slipped off the bed and staggered away to the pot. A biting chill was fast filling my blood. I saw a tarn in a ring of ice peaks, fed by age-old glaciers, drip drop, drip drop, the snowmelt seeping into the steaming pool was already a scorching unending gush by the time it flowed out of my body, making me swoon and hold to the walls. And like this, standing with legs apart dropping a burning watery arc into the pot, it came to me, the truth of things, that dignity was possible only in exile, outside the cataclysmic rumble of history, away from the inferno of desires and follies, this lust of the head to create, to vanquish, to enjoy, to suffer.

Suddenly, my head went clear, and there rose in the mind's eye shining above the green rolling hills the long and spacious marble stairway, and past it, as if floating in the air, the Pavilion of Solitude, to which I knew I would soon be leaving.

V

DO YOU see how cleanly they fall in place, one after another, subsuming the four cardinal points, these days and nights of our life? Always the same day, always the same night. The world nothing but a motif threaded with light and dark spaces, a simple, ineluctable result of the constant flux in the realms.

At first, only this. Elements, emptiness, meaningless movement. A vast unending terrain waiting to be taken, ordered, made intelligible. Then someone comes and draws a fence, marking a territory. Another maps the heavens, fixing the constellations, and little by little the universe begins to breathe, there arises a field of thoughts and possibilities. What baffling possibilities! What incredible schemes! In time, others follow, inducement is already at work in so new a world. Before long a giant web has come into place, is hanging from the farthest orbs into our lives, twisting its filmy yarns around our actions, enmeshing us, growing tighter, more intricate, with every move, every word.

Now it is never the same day, and seldom the same night. The phantasms of the human have been wholly projected onto the inhuman. Yet uncertainty and elusiveness are our lot, pain and beauty, fear and aggression our only markers. Somewhere there is peace too, a little of it, though more can be had with a slight enterprise. For this it is essential to conquer distant lands and civilize the barbarians inhabiting them. Thus, men happily tilling the fields are removed from their hoes and handed out swords, fields they have just begun to love and were about to fill with seed, fields they have recently snatched in an ongoing tussle from the grasp of unbearable darkness which exists between mammoth trees. But it is not for them to decide, the ruler's will must be done.

They are taught to repel attacks and strengthen defences. Finally, having been taken into the king's employ, simply by making them bow to a silhouette on one of the high terraces of the palace, so far up he must surely be in confidence of the gods, use must be found for them, for all the rage and ruthlessness that has been carefully crammed into their hearts. Soon armies are being drawn up regularly against each other, attacking and defending by turn, mostly at war, or else restless for war, a vast clumsy monster, bent on slaying, destroying, pillaging, dying on its way to everlasting peace.

But amid all this how do melancholy kings grown weary and indifferent to their own wars distract themselves on leisurely evenings? How do they sublimate into a harmless pastime their horrid past forever thrusting itself into the present? What is it that keeps them utterly engrossed in their terraced gardens and filigree palaces as they await despatches that will tell them nothing but the ruin of this or that enemy's troops at the hands of their savage warriors, long ago loosed on distant, unsuspecting lands?

Whose ingenious idea could it have been? Or did successive monarchs, logicians, artists, add to their ancestors' collective labours to devise this game played on a field which holds light and dark together, entire nights and days, change, choice, difference? Very like this earth of ours, spinning eternally in the shadow and fire of stars, taking us along while we draw our tiny wills against each other to create the play of life, to divert ourselves as we move from day to night, from night to day. For what else is the sublime and the ordinary, indeed the heart and the frontier of consciousness, but play?

Observe, then, the sixty-four squares, the thirty-two pieces, the four teams restless to clash, bands of elephants, chariots, horses, and footmen ready to defend their kings, complete chaos and carnage waiting to erupt at a roll of the dice.

VI

THE PLANT, its roots buried in a lump of soil, which Misa carried among her few belongings from those distant lands, has taken root beautifully, higher up, in the interior of the island, there a small section of the royal estate has been given over to its cultivation, the climate being suitable, sun tempered with cloud. Misa, the king's young companion throughout the long, arduous journey back to the island, little Misa from the roof of the world, the land of gods, godly land, godsland. The place, blue, white, and brown its dominant colours, so distant it begins to seem unreal only after a day's walk, a place shielded by the mighty Himalaya and the immensity of the lands they stare upon, lands of mythic rivers and lush jungles. Himalaya, the laughter of Rudra. Sparkling sheet upon sheet of snow suspended from the sky like a white illusion. What could lie past it? The king, staff in hand, pack on back, always two steps ahead of Misa, one shoulder bare, from the other hanging the hide of a leopard right down to the thighs, held tight by a cord round the waist, treading past everlasting snows, along flimsy passes that skirt unthinkable chasms. Two black dots in the vast terrain, here inching toward the white crest of a mountain, there descending into a vale of mist, beyond which lies nothing but more snow, more scree, bare jagged rocks piercing a thick coat of ice where not even eagles perch. The queen, awaiting the king's arrival on the hither side of this white wall against which even the sea winds are helpless, unable to cross, they fold and collapse into heavy showers over the forested plains. Green, white, and then beige, this is what the creator ordains, for this is what he saw, dreaming for a billion years while earth and wind went about his bidding. Prehistoric glaciers that glint like nickel in the noon air, rising from pinched crevices to sprawl along entire mountain sides, face to face in majestic solitude, past a thousand suns, with the celestial night. The plant, the only symbol, perhaps the last reminiscence of the land. The land, forbidden to all but the fiercest of adepts, where the king roamed for years, an ascetic. The queen, seeing at last the bluish black summits with such clarity it could only be a vision, pure and undiminished by distance. The plant, glowing green in the morning sun above a circle of cloud, its leaves plucked and rolled, then passed through pine smoke, brewing in a spouted urn. The hot, amber liquid with a delicious smoky aroma falling into the queen's bowl. The board, set for a match, armies drawn close in its four corners, each commanded by a king, complete with his quadripartite force, the elephant, the chariot, the horse, the infantry. The queen, having become addicted to the brew, sipping from the bowl before her. The scent, never failing to uncork the past, which makes the sun melt and sizzle all over it before pouring its molten light into the blackening vast like a waterfall. Maybe this is what makes her an addict, the wish to live this grand sight again and again. The sea breeze, moving blue and white triangular flags high up on the turrets and bastions. The sentries, spears and escutcheons in hand, stiff and silent under the fluttering flags, staring at the frozen landscape before them. Sand, stars, sun, waves. Wind forever churning the sea's face white and green, bending the trees, rustling the leaves, drawing a dry crackle from the cloth turning on itself above their ears, the only proper sound for a sentry's ears, a sound which tells him that peace reigns in the land, that he performs his task well simply by feeling the wind on his hardened face. Wind in the flags, flags in the wind, at once near and far from the world, pure phenomena inviting you to see its plain truth, that it is just this, a mind observing its own nature, a mind *capable* of observing its own nature, a mind which moves the flag, a flag which unleashes the wind, and thus, everything, nothing.

The boats in the docks, bumping into one another, producing a delicious wooden sound, sound made all the more delicious by the water. The lion heads on the trapdoors at the bottom of the towers, imitating the inscrutable expression of the sentries above, gold rings hanging from their jaws, which so many hands have pushed and pulled to open or close a passage of thick stone steps, weathered and shining from the weight of countless hurrying bodies over the years, to the ramparts above. The king, lost in a brown, cold immensity, growing less and less mortal with each day, for he is fast losing the sense of time and self, was this not why he came here?, this seeker of immortality, now fording the river on his way back to the cave from collecting twigs for firewood and nettles and berries, the only food which can be found anywhere for miles. But today he also has a gazelle hanging about his shoulders, its eyes open and lifeless, as if staring across the king's nape, awed and stupefied, into the gold and russet landscape. The river, its water ice cold and fast flowing, making its long, winding passage through the stark panorama of the desert, leaving a thin deposit of gold between the king's toes as he wades through it. The king, an ascetic. The ascetic, a sage. The sun's rays, slicing the chill air swishing past his shoulders as it forms and deforms dust into rock and rock into rubble to enter and tinge the skin a deep copper. The two travellers, huddled round the small fire they have kindled in a cave just above the pine forests, which at last rise up sharply along the mountain sides to reach them. The king, thoughtfully chewing the hard crusted bread while the child prepares the stew over the low blue flames that hiss and groan, starved for air that they are, and project dancing shadows on the black slate walls of the cave. The cave! This narrow, gloomy space, where light and dark interact in a thousand ways and the most complete manner, here the opposites merge and are made whole, here the inexplicable finds silent expression, here, in its warm depths, lions, thinkers, and seekers make their refuge. Misa, now almost a woman, the queen's daughter, friend, and confidante from the moment she reached the island and gave into the queen's open hands her own little hands clutching the small red pot with slim, pointed animals moving round it in the finest brushwork of black she has ever seen, raising the bowl of tea to her lips as she watches from across the board the queen feel the dice protractedly between her curled fingers. The queen, wishing for the throw to be a *five* or at least a *three* so she may begin the game at once, if not the pawn, then surely the horse may be leapfrogged into battle, for no more can she tolerate this painful matter with the dice, this tiny cuboid making the will hostage to chance at every step of the game, taking it away from its natural, intelligent course to strange, unforeseen ends. The dice, reducing the incorporeal to matter by way of a clever and simple association, what will we not do to make tangible, to see, touch, and grasp even the most ethereal and therefore the most significant of symbols. The spy, despatched by the exiled prince to take the message of imminent freedom to his wife enduring captivity in the heart of the enemy's kingdom, furtively jumping the fence into the palace courtyard. The travellers deep in the forest, turning back to look above the serrated line of the pines at the mountain peak which just yesterday was a never ending ocean of mist, and today is all but the tatters of a cloud flying from it, what better proof of the eye's deceit, of our smallness in the vastness of the world? The king, walking once more under the dense cover of trees after what seems a lifetime, is a lifetime. The child, unable to believe her eyes, for she has seen nothing like this before, not just a tree, which in itself would have been too much to take in, but an entire evergreen forest rising rapidly in every direction to claw the glistening snows of great massifs. The woman on the bridge, looking at the boats in the dock, shivering in the scarlet light of the setting sun, thinking of a man long dead. The cartload of grain, wheels clacking across the flagstones on its passage from the granaries to the bazaar, accompanied by the joyous shouts and jumping of children. The tall white stallion, grey veins visible across its full round belly, galloping away with its cloaked rider through the wet morning air of the forest, which mixing with the hot, excited breath of the animal forms a pale, flowing ring around them, joining the two in pursuit of a lasting, noble silence. The queen, standing in the balcony, watching the darkness which is the sea. The sage, eyes fiery, frame tall and bony, of an unkempt and matted mane, tufts of beard curling under the chin, skin dark and leathery, covered in dust and wood smoke of sacred fires, fording the icy river with a gazelle in the crook of his arm. The gazelle, bending in submission before the sage, and then up close, swiftly jumping into his open arms to lick the droplets off his chest and face. The gleaming blade, slowly sinking through the flesh of a supine figure, somewhere in the maze of the gold city.

VII

HOME AT last, and yet terribly homesick. This island, this city of gold, cleverly wrested from his stepbrother after long planning and a fierce political, even a brief physical, battle, this seat of his vast empire, which extended out to include faraway continents at the end of the ocean, as also large parts of the peninsula in the north, where after years of quashing rebellions and forging multiple alliances, the king had been able to gain control of territories as far up as the mouth of the Indus to the left, near which he had seen and fallen in love with the queen, and the delta of the Ganga to the right, whence it sprawled out into marshlands and forests before meeting the sea, this island where winds from all directions, carrying a variety of scents and climates, converged to ruffle the flags of his rule high above the palace, this land of his birth and triumph, of his education and wandering, where in times past he moved now like a philanderer, now like a sage, this earth of lush forests and groves where he first received the words of the holy scriptures from his father, the sage Visravas, descended from the great Pulastya himself, one of the ten mind-born sons of Prajāpati, the Progenitor, the First Born and the First Sacrificed, the Absent-Present One, and poured oblations into the sacred fire for the gods, was this home? Or was home in the forever changing flow of notes, of the myriad nuances and pitch oscillations, that rose up to enliven the air from his lightning-fast fingers holding the strings to the frets of the long, heavy lute resting across his chest, it seemed, in several places all at once? Nor was home in the hymns of the Sāma Veda, carefully selected and calibrated to recall the sound that created the universe, which, if one was attentive, could easily be heard in the vibrations of a bowstring. And what of the sacred rituals and sacrifices, which he had patiently learnt over the years only to later unlearn with ever more persistence and fortitude? Surely, home was not the queen, consort, or the child, nor the dice that moved one through night and day to victory or doom. Home was something else entirely, a tiny transparent spot somewhere behind the eye past which one entered into unending space shining with light. Home was the desert, the lake, the mountain. A land of few shadows. Home was where the wanderer felt the cold, crackling wind without judgment, where he saw, forgot, remembered again, ancient rocks becoming ever harder in their losing tussle with the elements, where the light filled wings of black-necked cranes against the chain of the peaks, the indifferent stare of the eagle swooping down on its prey, the leopard's sprint along the river, the red outline of an ibex balanced on a cliff edge caught in a flaming full moon, the tinkling of distant bells, crystalline constellations that stood out sharply one moment and were cosmic dust the next were the impressions that washed over him, filled him with a feeling he had not known before, of a joyous vertigo, if it could be described thus, of falling into the swirling flux and recovering anew to pure breath, pure movement. This perhaps was home then, which each passing moment was now fast taking away.

Within hours of his arrival, the news had spread throughout the capital, and from then on the gaiety could not be checked, whether in the palace or the market square a wave of expectancy and happiness made people delirious. For the moment, squabbles, spats, vendettas were forgotten and all rejoiced in a feeling of pride, camaraderie, and, if one looked deeper, stupidity. The king had returned to his subjects after a long absence, having achieved whatever it was he had set out to achieve. The most powerful of empires had the most powerful of men back on the throne. This was what made the citizens elated, an elation at whose bottom lay conceit, a conceit that stemmed from a certain misplaced conviction in one's superiority as a people, a belief toward which each of them had contributed by way of being ignorant, dogmatic, brave or cowardly in life or battle.

In the festivities that broke over the isle, the king was the most distracted of participants. And because he was distracted, he rarely grew impatient. Scarcely had he stepped out of a long bath than the royal priests were upon him, covering him up in a heady mixture of incense smoke, flower rings, and ceaseless chanting. And then, even before the queen could intercede, someone among the courtiers, with a love of ceremonies, had suggested a second coronation to mark the homecoming. Others in the group leapt at the suggestion, loudly affirming their support, only if to quell the ennui that is second nature to those who don't have to earn their bread out in the open. But by now the king had grown distant and deaf to everything. And because this was so, the proposed coronation went ahead. Again the tiger skin was laid on the ground before the throne, again the sovereign walked across it in three measured steps in a rite recalling the three steps of the Deity incarnate traversing earth, heaven, and hell, as if with such a trivial performance alone one came to resemble the Lord of three worlds. One by one, the sparkling, colourful rings were slipped back on his fingers, which had not yet lost the harshness of his roving, ascetic days. Where not in the so distant past was only his topknot of tangled hair, there now came to rest the heavy, bejewelled gold crown. Evil lurked beneath this opulence everywhere, glittered through this cornucopia of colour, the useless bounty of riches, madness of ages, revealed itself in the elegance of the damasks and draperies, in the tip of the priest's finger marking his forehead with a daub of vermilion, in the finely carved cornices, in paintings and tapestries that covered the long, shadowy walls, in the form-drenched pilasters projecting into the assembly hall from eight directions, in the din of tom-toms and clarinets, in every whiff of smoke that rose from repeated offerings into the sacred fire, in the perfume of flowers, casual smiles, ebullient voices, above all, in this velvety air of the make-believe. Home at last yet terribly homesick, the king felt like a monster trapped in a gilded maze of his own making.

And yet he had come back. But why? Because we never stop to think. Because we are incapable of stopping at all. Because we are obliged to move fast. Because endless possibilities confound us at each turn. Because our curiosity remains insatiable nevertheless. Because the trace can never be erased. Because life is a storm, a whirlwind, a lammergeier spreading its mammoth wings, coming at us at breakneck speed, and even when we run away from it, we run straight into it, tumbling down we go into the dark mouth opening to swallow us.

The queen watched silently from the side. The queen saw the proud bearing as before, the aloof pose monarchs affect to grace occasions such as these, for this, too, is one of their tasks, to please gods and subjects alike at the slightest opportunity, to regale them with food and drink, and in return receive the favour of one and the veneration of the other. That is the prescript of the ancients to the exalted one, which he is well advised to observe from time to time. But the queen saw something else too, which no one had seen. The queen saw the child she had never known, serene, innocent, supreme in his solitude, the watcher who could lose himself in the crush of cross currents of thought and action and not know it, who had somehow grown up to become his diametrical opposite, a fiercely astute and ambitious young ruler, bent on accumulating land and riches, more and more matter, anything that could be touched, controlled, consumed, enjoyed. The queen saw much more, but the queen still did not see all.

Then it happened suddenly. The king cast a glance at her, and the suspicion was confirmed. There was in that look something utterly alien to the gay surroundings, at first instance, merely a trifle bored, a trifle unsettled, but because the angle was right, and because in the complex geometry of shifting planes, the angle alone is the pathway to truth, she saw in those eyes a stirring that bespoke of events to come, events of which even the king was unaware, events that would change everything and reveal the past in a different light.

Now the formal ceremony was over, and the wine was flowing freely. This was the moment the king had been waiting for. Soon the revelries would turn into orgies and the licentious behaviour would know no bounds. He briefly spoke to the queen, and left the hall.

He moved fast through the long, twisting corridors, perhaps from habit, perhaps from unease. In his room he removed all the finery, threw a simple shawl over his shoulders, and walked to the corner where hidden from the eye lay a trapdoor. Past this deception was a flight of steps, which soon enough opened into a cool, broad, ill-lit tunnel cut in stone. The passage ended in a barn behind the eastern wing of the royal stables. From there he could mount a steed of his choice, and trot through the gates into the street, as the best disguise for a king is simply to cast off his regalia and dismiss the entourage, for how many subjects ever get a chance to see their king from up close.

He came to rest in a grove in the forest. From its edge flowed a brook where he dismounted. Here, far away from everything, he retraced in his mind the onerous happenings of the day. He decided to not return until later, to stay and build a fire. He took the axe from the saddlebag, and directed it at the fallen trunk of a tree. In the instant the axe was laid to rest, the jungle returned jumping and thumping to reclaim its place and sounds, the stream's gurgle, leaves rustling, shriek of a monkey, birdcalls, even the calm movements of the horse fell through the space and once more made it full. The jungle again was everywhere and everything, not a thought, not a movement remained which was alien to it, did not originate with or depend on it. In this place, where the sun couldn't break though with all its intensity, the trees constantly dripped with moisture. Lying on his back, the king gazed at a piece of sky through the waving mesh of pine needles, kept warm by the fire crackling in the cone of logs near him.

Meanwhile, in her new private quarters inside the palace, the child had fallen into a heavy sleep, at first dozing fitfully, continuously rolling from one nightmare to the next, twisting her closed face into grimaces and sweating profusely, but in time, as the fatigue spread evenly across her body, softening the visions, the hallucinations dispersed, and she floated into complete darkness.

When the king awoke, he could not immediately gather where he was or how much time had passed. At his side, a few embers still glowed amid the ash heap, deepening and paling as the breeze moved through them, while above stars sparkled in the sky against the grey of the pines. The horse stood still, watching. The forest was quiet. Only the endless murmur of the stream. Then another sound. Light, hesitant footfalls. Then, silence. Just the stream. Then a second, different sound mixed with the first, barely detectable. A doe is lapping up water. A soft golden light filters through the trees, covers its form in a faint halo. Somewhere a night bird breaks into song. He moves closer but the doe does not budge, not even when he spreads his fingers through its coat. The doe looks on with wide liquid eyes, arches its back, and rubs its ear against his chest. Then, all of a sudden, it moves away and hops off. Enjoyment, better to leave it before it leaves you.

A calm sweeps over him, and he knows he will in time return *home*. Until then, he will carry out the role given him, waiting patiently for the seasons to pass.

Seasons will pass, but not without leaving their residue, and who can tell whether patience alone would be enough in the end to further his resolve along desired lines? Caught in the rapids, events like so many waves will raise him to the crest one instance only to shove him into the swirling spray the next, sooner or later will eat into his reserve, and in pain, in exhaustion, in anger, in fear, will he not become one more senseless man among many, drowned by the clamour of the multitude? The loftier your position, the faster you went down. For vertigo was unsparing at great heights. Only high up, at the very centre of things, did you begin to feel the full weight of destiny which was little more than the countless squirming wills you had subjugated or influenced over the years that now, as dusk fell, drew in like menacing shadows to take you into their fold forever.

The king returned to the palace in the third part of the night, and proceeded straight to the queen's quarters. As he entered, he saw her reclining against the bedpost, and his figure at the door took her by surprise. What then passed between the two was ancient, pure, and simple, purged of all the needless emotions that one may, befitting his station, put to better use in the harem or the brothel. The king moved closer. But the queen held her place, impassively watching him close in, after how many years?, the slight distance between them.

It was thus that the three-night-long coitus began.

VIII

THIS IS a waste of time, dear Misa, a child's ludo really, said the queen, dropping the dice she had been quietly turning between her thumb and forefinger into the empty bowl before her. It fell straight into the bowl's concave bottom like a piece of lead, or so much dead matter, partly because it was slightly oblong and not a perfect cube.

For some time they had been sitting silently before the unopened game. Between them, as usual, lay the large board of sixty-four plain squares, set for a match, armies drawn close in its four corners, each commanded by a king, complete with his quadripartite force, a veritable image of war. The elephant, the chariot or the ship, the horse, the infantry. Everything was like before. Issuing from each of the four angles of the board, covering eight squares, in the front the four identical squat pieces, denoting the foot soldiers, and behind these the king, the elephant, the horse and, to the extreme left, in the crook of the angle, the chariot. Red was the colour of the warriors in the east, green of those in the south, in the west was stationed the yellow army, while the black held the north. Each king restless for victory over the others, the object twofold, first, to capture the square of the king commanding the army on the opposite top corner, thereby gaining an ally, and second, using the now combined force to slay the two adverse kings, and emerge victorious, reigning as supreme emperor.

Yet play had not commenced.

Previously, having settled before the board, Misa had waited for the queen to begin the game. The first few moments passed quickly without either of them realizing that the dice was still between the queen's fingers, and that she seemed to be giving some consideration to this simplest of acts, simple because what flowed from it was beyond their control and reckoning. When after a whole minute, they were still waiting, she started to grow impatient, wishing to intervene, and yet did not. Instead she kept looking now at the queen, and now at the board, telling herself, hold on a moment, just one moment, look it is about to happen, see, see, the fingers are loosening, an experience so real and paradoxical, the experiencer simultaneously crowning and annihilating *time*, that before long she had begun to relish the waiting, forgetting herself and her surroundings, and sinking deeper into a stasis from which she wished not to recover. The first conscious pause in a life which had been until then only movement, swirling and swooning in a river rush of motion, it was intoxicating, this instantaneous peace, this mental vacuity miraculously spreading to the very edge of her fingernails. On the board, the pieces stood frozen, their shadows clashing and quivering each time a cluster of clouds scudded across the sky.

Meanwhile, the queen was thinking. Is this a model of war? Could it not be improved further? But how and what for? Freedom, freedom, grant me some freedom, and I will show you what for! What an idea! Doubting the perfection of the ancients! These cleverly contrasting and unique movements of different forces, this delicate harmony of numbers in a most suitable alliance with the geometry of angles, the perfect weight and beauty of the pieces which when lifted between the fingers transmitted a charge to the head, and united you with a chunk of carved wood in an inexplicable way, creating altogether a dazzling array of possibilities, and releasing in the player a jet of joy which could be experienced nowhere beyond the square field of the game, could this be bettered?

But there then was the dice, making intelligence hostage to its throw at every step. And this in spite of the old taboo against games of chance, which inevitably led to gambling. Yet this most ancient of prohibitions was passed over, indeed, what was unthinkable, the great texts themselves sanctioned its use in the present case. A clear signal at the crucial role fate played in deciding the course of battles and empires. Armies clashed, warriors moved, but not without the invisible shackles of destiny round their ankles. Through the agency of the dice, the very gods entertained themselves, while the players were reduced to helplessly push wood, at least until skill and strategy were nearly useless in deciding victory or ruin. A most natural and inevitable system. For what has will alone ever achieved? No, the game was perfect, every alternative had been looked at from all sides by generations of players, warriors, and philosophers, the effect of every component on the collective whole thoroughly examined. No, one could so much as tinker with it.

But perhaps one could. Just a little. Nothing added or removed from the board, of course. But how about a slight realignment, a consolidation of forces? Don't we already play as if the opposite army was an ally, each player commanding not one but two sets of forces? Haven't we between us anyway dispensed with the tedium of four players tiring each other out before the real contest may begin? Why then we must join the forces at the start itself, and draw up the armies face to face, looking straight at one another, as on a battlefield. In the very least, it would open more space. More space without removing a single piece from the board? An illusion, a deceit of the eye, and yet how utterly real, necessary, and advantageous. Whoever heard of four armies clashing at random with each other. That is not war, that is mayhem. On top of which you could seldom plan and move at will. The dice! The dice! The dice!

The two opposing strains of thought had long enmeshed the queen. They had consumed not just the past half hour, but ran back months, maybe years, and had now found sudden expression against her conscious wish, as if some strange impulse, unable to hold on further and resolving the matter of itself, had forced her hand.

But there was hardly anything new about this mental dialectic. It was the same old conflict rearing its head in the most rigid of places, namely, rules of play. The same old vacillation between following ancient precepts and discovering for oneself, beliefs one had grown up with which had dwindled before events, desires, choices that forced one to see differently, between tradition and especial insight, between the steadily gathering press of fate and the strong, if fitful, resistance of the will.

Let us do things differently for once, continued the queen, quite unaware of how much time had passed since she had first picked up the dice, and quite forgetting her strange and unexpected previous assertion. But before that you must relay back to me the rules of play. Everything as if you were initiating me into the game. All that the queen wished before putting her thoughts into effect was simply to hear in another voice, coming from outside of her, rules that had already been made more or less redundant in her head, so as to confirm and fix their absurdity for anyone who cared to see, and thus absolve herself from the wound she was going to inflict upon the heart of age-old principles.

Quickly coming into her element, the sudden stasis all but forgotten where now only suspense gathered with each passing moment, such is the fate of even our noblest of experiences, the constant consigning to oblivion of all that we see and feel in order to go on living, and without even a questioning glance, Misa, deftly tempering her rising interest with the right measure of respect, began to speak.

Four players, four teams, four kings, ready for their four-pronged attack. The throw of the dice. A cuboid, marked with *two, three, four*, and *five*, respectively, on each of its longer sides, *six* and *ace* being of no use here. Each number a clarion call for one or another piece to proceed. So if the throw turned up *five*, either the king or any of the pawns moved, if the throw be *four*, the elephant, if *three*, the horse, and if *two*, the ship or the chariot entered the field. The king moved one square in any direction, the pawn, one square straight forward, but struck the enemy through either angle, in advance. The elephant moved, so far as its path was clear, in the direction of any of the four cardinal points, while the horse leaped over three squares in an oblique direction. The ship, where it was not hindered by any piece, moved two squares diagonally. The ship and the pawns mutually captured each other, but could not take a superior piece. The king, elephant, or the horse, however, could capture any of the adverse forces at pleasure, but were themselves subject to be captured only by the king, elephant, or the horse of an adversary. Obviously, preserving the king was of utmost importance, and when either of the middle pawns had reached the opposite end of the board, it assumed the power of an elephant or the horse whose very square it had attained.

True, true, interrupted the queen impatiently, and yet the weakest flank of each army is opposed to its antagonist's strength, and the piece in each army which would be of most use on the flanks, is placed in a situation where its operations are cramped, and although it appears that two armies are allied against the other two, the inconvenience of their battalia remains in great measure. Besides, it also appears that each separate army has to guard against the treachery of its ally, as well as against the common enemy, for it is recommended, and allowed to either of the kings, to seize the throne of his ally, that he may obtain complete command of both armies, and achieve conquest for himself alone. And as if this wasn't enough, the use of dice to determine the moves is fatal to the true enjoyment of the game, where we often see the most consummate abilities defeated by chance, the queen's voice, excited, almost furious, rang higher than usual.

Sparing not even a glance to the help who had been standing in attendance all this while, oblivious to everything except orders, the queen asked for a spare set of pieces to be brought her. This being done, and without waiting for the other set to arrive or feeling the need to explain her actions, she began to remove the red and yellow warriors from the board. At last only sixteen remained, eight of green and eight of black, covering the two opposite corners, but facing each other.

When the handsomely carved sandalwood box was given her, the queen hastily removed the lid, picking out black and green pieces at random from among the red and yellow ones that together lay jumbled up deep in its purple silk insides, but deposited them carefully, symmetrically, green on this side, black on the far side, lingering over each shape, feeling every curve, every edge, as she left them over one by one in their newly assigned squares. In such lingering was a new burgeoning insight, henceforth every move would emanate from and depend on her, life or death was no mere chance now, not some abstract, distant consequence thrust on you by a tiny rolling stone, but fiercely personal, a matter of careful planning, strategy, skill and daring, and, thrust or parry, she alone were responsible for what would follow. Pieces which until then had been so much wood or ivory, presently assumed in her eyes a new importance, and she saw in them, for the very first time, the love and handiwork of families and generations of craftsmen, scores of them even now maintained on royal patronage, who, busy and bent in their dim crowded workshops, eye following the hand, hand following the eye as it marked light incisions across the neck of the wooden horse to depict its mane, or shaped into a four-petaled flower or jewel the tip of the king's crown, poured their artistry for days and months in sculpting these miniatures of inconceivable beauty. Theirs was an art reflected solely in their touch, here supple, leaving the lightest of impressions to depict the wind in the sails of a ship on move, there deep and piercing, to capture the precise look in the elephant's eye, keen but wary. Only now, only in the plan she had for them could these tiny warriors ever hope to measure up to the labour of their creators.

Once the queen's task was accomplished, there stood from left to right, along the entire width of the board, two vast armies looking at each other in place of four divided smaller troops, awkwardly positioned as it now seemed, in right angles to their neighbours. A wide empty stretch of squares separated the two conjoined forces, where the battle would soon take place. But just as she had done this, a thought came to her, and she swept the green pieces off the board with a gentle swing of her hand, replacing them instead with the yellow ones, yellow being the farthest colour from black among the three, at last a contest between true opposites.

For each team, in the middle, were the two kings, flanked on either side by elephants, horses, and, in the extremities, the ships or the chariots. And before them, closing the ranks, eight pawns or foot soldiers. Unconsciously, perhaps, this was the moment the queen had been waiting for. She promptly picked up the knife lying in the fruit platter close at hand, and with a swift short stroke slashed the tip of the crown of one of her kings. Repeating this gesture with the black piece, she at last looked up at Misa, who had been closely watching every move lest she drew a wrong inference, and, bending over the board, placed the piece back in its square with a sharp decisive thump, stating rather matter-of-factly, Here's the queen. Like her diminished crown, she has only half the powers of the king. She may proceed only one square diagonally around him. As of the rest, you know the moves, and there is the dice no more. An open space from left to right for a clean head-to-head engagement. And, for once, let's begin with you. Here pausing briefly so as to not appear too assertive, she remarked rhetorically, though also a bit uncertainly, Now then, shall we play?

But Misa couldn't move. Following everything, doing nothing. Stilled into inertia by the crushing weight of such vast unexpected freedom, she continued to gaze at the board, as if from far away. Free to choose, yet not daring to do so. Which of the ten pieces to push forth, she pondered, unable to decide. In her thoughts several possible openings one by one ran their course with lightning speed, petering out invariably into the ranks of the enemy troops. At best, she could see four or five moves ahead, after which all grew muddled, and she had to begin anew. This, however, was not the only difficulty. Hardly did she devise the first opening, *devise*?, could that be the word?, could it be anything but a studied randomness?, she became painfully aware of how pathetically one-sided and stillborn any strategy was bound to be, unless, of course, the other's progress into the game was matched step for step with a swift response, relentlessly rethinking, redeveloping, improvising one's plans to remain a step ahead of the opposition. Your thought soared briskly above the board where it engaged the adversary in a slow, imperceptible duel, each threading through the other's advances, striking and defending by turn, hot pursuits that could abruptly end up in blind alleys, weak spots that disappeared like mirages or lay carelessly open to attack like so many traps, thrusts repelled, forces redeployed. Movements, which had earlier appeared blunt and accidental, were suddenly sharp and vicious, gleaming with devilish intent, bent solely on slaying swiftly without thought or mercy. Previously the dice had dictated everything, and there was little need to think in advance. Tactics were more or less useless then. You moved in the manner chance decreed. But now the entire task fell on you, and how pitifully ill-prepared you were for it. With such meagre means at your disposal how could you ever begin to understand the full sweep of its complexity? Too much freedom was now concentrated in the square field of the board. It was unbearable. There was evil in this. Tremendous evil. One would never emerge unscathed from the game's pull.

Wind, which high up was rapidly making and dissolving clouds, had dropped entirely near the ground, and an unexpected chill prevailed in the air, inspiring the kind of sadness which assails you on certain afternoons as the year is drawing to a close, and the light turns crimson and the trees grow still and the tweeting of birds in the branches can be heard more clearly, and just for a few moments, but this you remember only later, you seem to mourn something you have lost, without knowing what it is.

IX

DA, DA, DA, is what the thunder said. *Damyata, Datta, Dayadhwam*, is what the Father meant by those resounding, recurring syllables. Thus also was he understood by his triad of descendants, gods, men, and demons, sitting by his feet on their last night of tutelage. Be self-controlled, said Prajāpati to the first, for the gods possessed enormous powers. Be giving, said he to the second, whom he knew could easily grow covetous. Be merciful, echoed the thunderclap one final time in the thickening night, for the dark ones were susceptible, on the flimsiest of grounds, to the most unusual bouts of passion or fury, something they might later have had cause to regret, for remorse is the other face, the dark back, of thoughtless action.

The lesson was over. The children were delighted. Bliss filled them, drowned their senses. Overjoyed, they looked at earth with longing, the first to teach discipline, the second to ennoble with charity, the third to grant mercy. In order to please the Father and do his bidding, they turned away from him. Nobody noticed that the Father was gone. As if he had never been, Prajāpati had dissolved into that which is neither space, nor time, nor matter. Undifferentiated, indistinct, eternal, he ruled without ruling. In front and behind him, within and without him, the firmament glowed with incalculable points of gold. Seven of these made up the shape of a plough or a dipper, the very symbols of fertility and nourishment, the Bear as some would later say, the never blinking, forever-watchful eyes of the great seers. They who came before the children. They who were born of the Father's mind. They, the Father's mind.

But like the teacher, the teaching was forgotten. It was bound to be. The world is like that. It enchants. Hardly there, beings succumb to its spell, drenched from top to bottom in the spray of phenomena. It is the goal, this spell, the mind at once engenders and strives for. The obstacle it wishes to overcome even as it forms it. The mirror it needs to know itself. This world cast in impressions of a dizzying variety, like an elusive antelope always a step ahead of the hunter's grasp, and separating them, surrounding them, this scent of the hunt, nothing but the hunt, until perhaps at long last the hunter pounces on the hunted and rolls over the edge with it into the one true, formless totality.

But how rarely does this happen, leaving the mystery of the world intact, fully cloaked in its manifestations. Only the hunt continues. Forever and ever. Its path rising from the earth into the dark vault of the sky, cutting through the stars, scattering along the way, for this is inevitable, countless bones and bodies.

Yes, blood, bones, bodies. This is what the wisdom of the thunderbolt had warned against, and this is what the listeners so easily forgot. As soon as they alighted upon the world, the children quarrelled. Coveting what did not belong to them, exercising neither restraint nor mercy, each cleverly selected a foe weaker than himself to pour out his fury upon in full. They tricked one another, they schemed and fought unendingly to no end, unless that end was simply to put on show and sustain the spectacle of life. At any given point in time one or more such battles raged in one or another of the worlds. Covered in soot and blood and abrasions, the children in due course came to resemble each other, as if the lines of distinction had ever been sharply drawn. Gods incarnating as men, men rising far beyond gods, who, if not men, were the great seers?, gods who were also demons, demons who were remarkably close to men, these happenings were not out of the ordinary. Yet not all was war. Incredible though it looked, peace still lay in the midst of wrath and death.

Men, who now placated the gods and now parleyed with the demons, had an ambivalent position. They held the mean between the two opposites, and so also held their peace the more easily, but if incited they could be a resilient group. Their allegiance swayed from one to another every once in a while. For although they believed gods to be the more powerful if not always the more even-handed, they felt a strange if somewhat tenuous camaraderie with the demons who being their neighbours on earth held with them several interests in common. And what was man and what demon, in the final analysis, was merely a manner of speaking. The other, the unknowable, the dark one, the demon. That was the simple chain of inference. For not all who were described thus were giants or inhuman monsters, not all were scoundrels or bullies. Nor were they bloodthirsty savages or cannibals.

Simple as this seemed, it was not simple enough for those upon whom fell the vicissitudes of living. For if there was a thing life fortified day in day out, as much in the small as in the big, it was prejudice. To live was to be prejudiced. Prejudice was the very marrow of our mental makeup. Dissociation was the technique with which we worked things out. Counting relied on this, words, too. So did every system and category of thought. Unless the eye separated, it saw nothing. And yet how awfully little it saw, and even what it saw it dissected, while life rushed unseen like a raging torrent behind the observer's back. Prejudice, fear, and the wish to dominate and annihilate the face of the other. The chase of the antelope. The hunt.

But never before had the children clashed like they did on the island far out in the sea, as if kicked out from the mainland, the island where the dark ones had built their alluring refuge surrounded by great tropical rain forests, the sparkling capital city, the seat of the demon king's vast empire. For eighty-four days, the terrible war continued on its accursed shore. Out there, as the sun slowly arced in the sky, dust flowed into sweat and sweat into blood, hands hurriedly grabbed the entrails let loose by the spear and tore them off in disgust to finish the task quickly before moving to the next adversary. Bones crackled like dry twigs going up in flame and men kept falling, sinking everywhere amidst a cesspool of bleeding flesh, piss, and vomit, whereas those still standing and moving were pale as ghosts, swathed in dust, shaking and eluding, with each turn of their bodies, Death which was wheeling in the oppressive air, entering willy-nilly the jaws of the wounded that clenched only too late and were already slackening and drooling as she made off with their life. Not once during this unremitting carnage did the thunder roll DA, DA, DA, DA, DA. Not one among them recalled the benign, sacred words of the scriptures, *Damyata, Datta, Dayadhwam.* Not one voice begged for mercy, not one hand trembled in horror at its own doing. Even the heavens remained clear, distant, glittering with stars, heavens that had clouded and flared and pealed so often in the past. Only the eyes of the great seers watched, stupefied. Night upon night, the Bear hung from the sky like a question mark over the abyss, as if the seers were asking in horror, Why? What for?

For honour. For avenging your honour. The demon king had contrived and abducted the exiled prince's wife, who had been ever since held captive in his palace, and whom the wicked king refused to release with due honour, even after entreaties and warnings to this end. The word again, honour. A man's dignity, a warrior's code of honour, had been ridiculed. What was there to be done? Lust and vanity had clouded the king's head, we said. The vile man must be taught a lesson, we declaimed. Too much evil only brings ruin, to war!, to war!, we cried in rage.

That for the sake of this very honour many ignoble deeds were also committed, nobody saw or thought it fit to recount. We didn't ask whether it formed a part of the warrior's code to inflict injury on a woman, unarmed and blindly enamoured of the prince? We didn't stop to think whether it was befitting a man, the second prince of an illustrious dynasty, to simply slice off the nose of this woman, the demon king's half-sister, likewise exiled and wandering in the forest, for merely rubbing her breasts against the younger prince's forearm? Of course, she had incited the brothers, first lecherously and when that didn't work by provoking their ire in trying to attack the docile wife of the elder prince, an attack more childish and futile than dangerous, doomed to failure by the very fact that she was alone, impoverished and empty-handed, without even a stick to arm her against the two ablest archers in the whole realm. But then too her anger had been aroused by their own doing, they played and led her on awhile, as she ran from one to the other, taking her chances with each and making a fool of herself. Indeed she may have had other evil motives in putting on show this pathetic act concocted in equal measures of desire and villainy, motives that had their beginnings in those obscure iron-blue depths of the heart that nobody has ever traversed to the end, motives that like silken threads tangled and untangled, until the whole sorry tapestry was lost in the gathering darkness of the deepest past. Or perhaps she was destiny herself come to meet the demon king from an earlier life, incite him to such base, no, for someone of his powers and intelligence, simply befuddling action so that he should pay for the wrongs done then or make good some ancient unremembered pledge. Honour, however, hardly could be the name of what erupted from the many non-rational springs of action and feeling of all those involved, a number so vast and indefinite none could have predicted it. Honour was not in being truculent and a little too free with your hands, not in the matter of that hanging nose dripping a steady flow of blood into the victim's convulsing bosom.

I was there, quietly passing my time in the forest, waiting for events to catch up with me, recalled the child in the old cedar. In the forests at the foot of the *Nilgiri*, the blue mountains that made up the western edge of the southern provinces, not much farther from the hill where I was born. Wind-born they told me, for a kite had flown away with a pinch of the divine pudding in its beak that fell straight into my mother's hands, and which she promptly transferred to her mouth taking it to be a blessing from heaven, a pudding that I later learnt was meant for the womb that would give birth to the exiled prince. God-incarnate, he was called. And so I became one of them, the gods. Life's affinities, you could say. Elective affinities. So it was I felt a spontaneous sympathy for the elder prince the moment I laid eyes on him, and so was I ready to do his bidding from the start, whatever it be, without doubt or indecision, although I wasn't then aware of the special connection that bound us together. The pudding, the kite, the breeze.

At the time I was living with the tribe that took the monkey as its totem. Its members went about wearing a crude image of the primate round their necks, and the tribe's triangular flags, too, were painted with something resembling it. The men were swift climbers of trees and could camouflage themselves on the spur of the moment. More than a few among them had developed this into an art form and were seen as sublime shapeshifters.

I had come to the tribe upon completing my instruction in the *Vedas* and certain esoteric practices that granted one the power to change form and move with ease over wind or water, this supreme knowledge transmitted then as now orally from teacher to disciple, one to one in strict confidence, whereupon my teacher asked me to join and aid the brother of the tribe's ruler who had also been his student in old days and had recently fallen on hard times, banished by the elder one, the ruler, for what he saw on the former's part to be an unpardonable act of betrayal and cowardice.

Another affinity, another exile. Exiled in your own home, a wilderness where others came from far away to serve their respective exiles. It seemed like the season of exiles.

When I met him he was living in hiding with a band of his followers in a cluster of rock caves with a system of underground streams. It was not the ideal place to live, for the rocks constantly dripped water the colour of rust, and it was wet and cold on most evenings. But the place offered protection in that it lay concealed in the darker part of a ridge with clear views of the forest in three directions and there was no lack of food or firewood. He was dejected and in utter despair, left with next to no self-esteem, for the elder brother had gone ahead and taken this man's wife as his own queen, following the tribe's custom. In there, accompanied by the sound of dripping water and the hiss of the flames sawing the darkness, I listened to the exile's tale of ruin and woe.

For some time an ogress had been carrying away women and children to her remote grotto. People came crying for help to the ruler who at once made off to beat the life out of her. The younger one offered to go with him. Near the mouth of the grotto, the ruler instructed his brother to watch and wait for him at the spot, and rushed into the darkness. He waited a long time and when waiting some more there was still no sign of the other, he sadly surmised that great evil had befallen his brother. Not a sound could be heard, not a howl, not a footfall. Dark thoughts gripped him and he felt heavier in his body and his shadow stretched long and trembling from his feet. Just as he was thinking what best to do, his sight fell on the ground where the mud had turned to a thick red gruel, fed by fresh drops of blood that were even then trickling out from the mouth of the cave. Dreading that his brother had perished, slipping and swaying half from fear, half from sorrow, he used all his strength to push a heavy boulder across the mouth of the grotto, buckling more than once under its weight, and returned to tell others the sad news. The very next morning he was proclaimed head of the tribe by consensus, and the same evening the elder one returned seething and quivering in rage with bloodshot eyes to find the deserter on his own throne, and assumed the worst.

In truth, the ogress had fled through a passage in the rocks while she was being pursued, and it was there, deep in the caverns, that she met her violent death. It was, in fact, the first of her thick blood that had sloped out from the mouth of the cave and had made the one waiting desperate, while the victor was negotiating one of the several passages that opened out from the accursed chamber and led straight to a dead end. By the time he stumbled upon the correct way he was much troubled, but his troubles were far from finished as he soon realized he had been bolted in quite thoroughly by the very person he had left behind to watch his back.

What was betrayal and cowardice to the other appeared to me from the exile's narration simply an error of judgment, entirely free from malice, although there was something of the cowardly about it. But we judge quickly and severely, forgetting that on him who waits each passing moment falls like a hammer and in the very act itself lie the seeds of its abandonment.

The punishment, notwithstanding the justness of the other's anger, was too harsh, and we decided to recruit an army of men to lead a rebellion against the arrogant ruler. But the recruitment went along pitifully. What could we offer to lure anyone into our foredoomed cause? For the ruler was feared in the entire realm as possessing supernatural strength and was famed for having beaten even the demon king in his younger days. Legend had it he had received a boon from a seer that his adversary's strength will fall to half against him in combat. Not many, therefore, could be found who readily espoused the cause of the rebellion or did not fear for their lives at the hands of the enemy. Mostly only outlaws and petty brigands were willing to join in the hope of a later booty or reinstatement into the tribe.

But those who had been recruited stayed away from the exile's loyal group, keeping company with their own kind and waiting for the incursion to begin. I kept a wary eye on them for they were day by day growing lazier from inactivity and dissipation. These were men whose entire lives were ruled by base drives and indiscipline, and all they looked forward to while they deferred even as they whetted their instinct for carnage was to eat and drink around campfires they built at night, telling tales which were little else than poorly culled and rehashed versions of the fables enshrined in the *Vedas*, and which they had picked up on their itinerant movements through the region from the mouths of tradesmen or gypsies whom they would first waylay and later rob and murder without a thought.

Fables, the same ones I had learnt with such care and patience, and whose real meaning not one among us could fully elucidate. Noble words which were sublime portents on a sage's lips, here in the depths of night were only quick, supple bearers of stories and myths that softened the terrifying possibilities of unbounded time and gave the half-lit faces of these rogues the vulnerable look of babes in cribs. Here as elsewhere, words, narratives, and consciousness were inextricably bound together so that speech seemed the prime refuge of souls loosed upon the impenetrable face of without.

Night after night, I heard them from the shadows of a sal tree, beyond whose sprawling branches curled the flames that lit up their faces from below as they squatted about the burning logs, constantly sputtering crimson rinds into the grey pillar of air, and passed clay pitchers around, telling stories by turn, till their eyes lost the fire in them and turned smoky and stood open for the night and whatever lay in its wake.

It was then, on one of my routine wanderings, that I came upon resting on a rock the exiled prince, who, along with his brother, was slowly making his way to the demon king's capital to rescue his wife. But how? Two warriors, no matter how able, were helpless against the vast strength of the enemy and his forces. And for a start they were not even certain of their way. I took them along to my friend's shelter, where the exiles met and exchanged their sad tales in sympathy and agreement, conferred at length, and finally sealed the historic pact, a solemn oath of exiles that would see wrongs done to each punished, iniquities put right, honour restored, virtue re-established.

The plan then was for my friend to go and challenge his brother to a duel and while they were assaulting and tearing each other apart, for the prince to shoot an arrow from behind a tree and kill the arrogant fool. Thus, not only his rightful position and his wife, but the entire kingdom would be restored to him, in return for which he would forthwith align his men and, with himself at the head of the troops, help the princes lay siege to the enemy's citadel and rescue the woman in captivity.

It was not much different from a coup d'état, though none of us saw it as such in our simple inflamed hearts bent solely upon avenging the wrongs done to each. The plan was both quick and effective. None saw anything but victory in it, none saw anything near abominable. Now there was little need of the irregulars we had been recruiting, and we left them sitting on their haunches girdling the burning logs, regaling one another with tales and drinks and laughter, to pick up on the morrow their violent lives from where they had left them, without once thinking of the lost opportunity. Nothing was unusual in this. Life was one such long chain of unfulfilled plans and discarded choices, and where one gate closed, ten others came open.

Surprising though it seemed, things went scrupulously to plan, even if there were delays and misunderstandings along the way. For when the exile had won back his wife and the kingdom besides after what seemed to him a cruel and extended period of hardship, he, as was only natural, wished to delay further travails and enjoy a little the pleasures of throne and community, until he was rudely pulled out from a night of carousing and squarely threatened by the younger prince. Very soon the tribal army was on the march through the forest, snaking its course toward the southern tip of the peninsula, having received along the way crucial guidance regarding the route it was to take.

More than a millennium had passed since then, and all the actors in that horripilating drama had long since turned to dust or something finer than dust. Past that epic war, past many great wars, only he remained, the child in the tree. Not a few hundred years, and already the events were being recounted as children's tales. Maybe that was why wars were fought, so that at some remote point in time they could be told as tales to children. Everything was possible here where no matter how slowly the wheel rolled it would get from blood to laughter soon enough.

Just the other day, while he sat above a huge rock beyond the spray of the falls, he had heard coming down the opening in the hills the voice of a woodcutter reciting the story to his little son astride a burro, utterly pared and simplified, as is the case with stories or the telling of them, the story of the demon king's death at the hands of the prince-in-exile, the former, in his telling, the embodiment of pure evil and the latter of pure good, a moral tale, a tale of morals. As if there ever was such a thing in life, as if what was cruelty to one was not kindness to another. Now all that remained was for a bard to come along singing it from village to village, improvising and embellishing it as he sang into history, Rama's journey or Rama's story, for one's journey was also one's story, the only story, no matter how and in how many ways one chose to tell it.

But not a word passed from father to son about that death on the battlefield at the very cusp of night, much like that of the demon king at the end, but nowhere near as significant to this story, the death on the close of the first day, the death from my hand, the death which occurred outside time, the unaccounted death, the death that could have been avoided if I had not been entirely beside myself clearing my way all day through bones, blood, bodies.

What to think of it? We are but trailing phantoms in another's story to say nothing of those who trail in ours.

The child turned suddenly to look at something. His pet puma had materialized on the branch as if out of thin air, and was now watching him with its yellow-green eyes. The child spread his arm round its neck to caress it from below. A low mist was rising over the trees in the east, but here the sun shone clear and the rays left a reddish tinge in the animal's coat. Far into the distance, at the rim of the world, blazed the immense, metaphysical wall of ice.

X

IT RAINED without cease for several days. The heavens were making good for the longest dry spell in years, for the most part of which the war had raged on.

Had it happened, we would probably not have noticed the gradual grading of the sky from blue to white to grey, the world darkening above us and feral sparks renting the cloudbank and the thunder rumbling DA, DA, DA, DA, DA, that a golden light was falling in bands far out in the sea, while here amidst the turmoil rain was upon us, churning and loosening up the mud under our feet, so that the solid ground beneath was soon a quagmire where mud not water dripped from our hair, silting in any cavity it could find, even working as a salve for our wounds.

But, of course, it did not rain, and the soil was kneaded solely with the sweat and blood from our teetering, faltering bodies. The sun burned stark and incandescent in the skies and drew out of the humid air a terrible effluvium of death and decay, against which bracing ourselves we went on thrusting and parrying until night fell, provisionally or for good.

Within hours from the start of the day's fighting, vultures were alighting on the corpses that lay strewn along the war ring. The birds would settle on the still bleeding warm flesh and begin at once to peck at the softer skin around the neck and the face or scoop out the eyes clean from their sockets and suck on them for all their worth. If the breath of war moved closer, they lifted their wings, even flapped them in slow, deliberate strokes a few times, but then having barely

risen would come down instantly to the free and generous repast
before them.

And rain it did not when the war was over, not when the throne
was no more vacant, nor when I took my siesta day after day,
smoking my pipe and watching the tiny, indigo-crowned birds
flitting in the hedgerows, threading fleeting lines of colour through
them, nor when the long and spacious marble stairway and then the
pavilion itself swam before my eyes.

The sky was high and clear above the yard when the stable boy
brought in my horse, bridled and groomed, the leather saddlebags,
holding a few personal effects and provisions for the journey,
hanging from each side of the seat. But not before I was deep in the
forest did it occur to me for the first time, so much had the war, its
preparation and the resulting exhaustion, made us neglect, how long
it had gone without rain.

Prancing on they went all day long, the traveller and his horse,
mixing their breath with that of the trees, leaving a white plume in
their wake and filling the world to the brim with the continuously
unrolling, untiring clickety-clack of their movement, elated at this
sudden freedom, consuming all earth and all time, until
unexpectedly they emerged from the forest and the rider reined in
his horse and the horse reared and neighed, and the rider saw the
pavilion, issuing like a flame above the earth at the extreme end of
a path that went crawling into a distant hill. A lone band of light was
washing over it where it stood towering and radiant on the
escarpment, while in every concavity about shadows were
gathering, swooping down straight from the fast flowing clouds
which were closing in on the sun from every direction. Even better,
thinks the man, even better than how I envisioned it. And then the
last ray of light was snuffed out and night came on suddenly.

By the time the rider ascended the hill, rain was upon him. A
cloudburst. Birds had flown away, all life had retreated into the
bush. Torrents gushed down the slopes and through the trees and the
entire country sank in a deluge of rain, out of nowhere an enormous

lake appeared that would slowly come to cover everything. Thunder struck and gales blew. Shielding his eyes against the downpour, he went trotting up the path that blazed white, pink and ochre by turn in its swift dissolution, reflecting the wrathful face of the firmament, in a torrid landscape where none moved save he. There was nothing to tell if he had in fact seen the building or it was merely a vision engendered by a mind reeling from tiredness, hope, and yearning. But onward he went, soaked to the bone and shivering from the sharp drop in temperature.

Around halfway up the hill as the track made hairpin bends, I could make out tiny lamps or flames being lit one by one, like the first stars appearing from the gauze of dusk, and toward them I went, a weary traveller riding this constellation of lights as a guide to the end, never letting it out of my sight, although the slanting rain and the curving, melting road and the hair plastered over my face made this difficult.

Upon dismounting, a searing pain shot from the soles of my feet, up through my legs, collecting and pinching in the small of my back. I suddenly noticed how modest this place was, how utterly unlike what I remembered of it. The rain was at work in the front lawn which was untended and slipping into ruin and wilderness. The marble steps, maybe ten or fifteen, not more, neither too wide nor too high, nothing like how I had dreamt them, but fixed solidly to the ground, paling and coming apart on the edges. This was just an old hunting lodge slowly falling into decay from lack of interest or forgetfulness. Long ago, the dead king had passed it on to me in a kind and spontaneous gesture after we had returned from a successful hunt one evening. Often had I thought of the place, but not once had I returned. One thing or another kept happening, whether at the court or out in the field, delaying my decision. Later I had even thought of bringing Misa here for a day or two, but I could never garner the courage to ask her, and besides is one ever sure about love?, either it is too quick in coming or it is too late, and in both cases calamitous for the parties involved. Better it would have been for the poets to never sing of love, for then maybe we would not have discovered it within ourselves. Soon anyway the events took a turn for the worse and war was upon us. Yet I was glad to have come now, if only alone and vaguely grieving.

Three men had emerged from the pavilion's dim interior onto the main landing to see about the traveller. This was what remained of life here. Maybe this was what always remained once the king and his escort had departed after the excursion. Three shadowy forms floating in a parallelogram of flames issuing from the half-damaged, serrated urns on sills and parapets that had yielded their colour piecemeal to time and the elements, time which here was nothing but the elements. Solitary men getting by in age, half slaves, half hermits. What did it mean to them, the war and the subsequent change of power, the weariness of loss? Probably they were not even aware of it, content with collecting food and wood in the forest, watching the sky, listening to the streams, brewing their ale, and smoking and drinking each evening round the low fire. Days alike, empty and peaceful. At most a careful barter of words and movements to sustain them. A bare life, a routine life, a robust life.

One man came down the steps and led the horse away to the stables at the rear of the building, another rushed inside to light the fire and prepare a meal, while the third stood right there, calmly waiting for me at the edge of the steps. They seemed to behave most naturally, as if they had been expecting me, after these many years, on this of all evenings, when the night was bursting with thunder and rain.

On the landing under the roof, the attendant took the dripping cloak off my shoulders. Did he recognize me? I turned and from the sanctuary of softly waving flames watched the sheets of water being ruffled by the wind and charge leaking from the sky and flaring up the night with its deep staccato roar. I could have stood there for hours, watching and hearing the rain, not thinking about anything, forgetting the past and its ties to me.

I changed into dry clothes and settled by the fire, supping from an earthen bowl a hot creamy broth made of goat's fat and hooves along with unleavened bread with burnt rings that left a faint taste of ashes on the palate. It was an appetizing fare. Afterward, someone handed me a pipe stem and I settled down with the others drinking and discussing, in words that barely broke away from the long pauses that held them, the day's few and common happenings prior to my arrival. The rain drummed lightly afar and the fire crackled from the twigs bursting in flames, releasing a smell of juniper in the spreading warmth. I knew not when sleep levelled with me and when it left me far behind.

Sometime before dawn, the first dawn, the second or the fifth, it was forever dawn, a pallid, rain-sodden dawn, I had a dream. I saw my elephant, not dark and lacerated in the shed when I had last laid eyes on him, but snow-white, like Indra's ride Airavata, with three, four, even five heads, falling from a bluff into a cold blue luminosity, spinning as it fell in slow motion, without a sound, trailing away in his vast bulk into the gap opening under my feet.

We were four friends, all warriors, what else could we be, men chained to their humble, uncertain origins. Men who, to begin with, did not possess even the comforts of a blacksmith or a potter. Men who had taught themselves early the art of survival in the street, who only knew how to handle weapons or swing their limbs fast in combat. To then be recruited into the king's army seemed like good fortune. Food, handsome weapons, a roof over the head, however temporary, some coins to buy drinks each evening, and fresh clothes on the back. This was no small fortune. In return for which we were simply to practice the one skill we knew, and this time without fear of sanctions for the deed was to be done in the name of law or defending the nation's honour. Eventually, two ended up in the ranks on foot, one in cavalry, and I on the elephant. Ours was a bond formed in the early days of scarcity and hardship, from before my ascension to the higher echelons of the court, something which the passage of time, or what was in my case the accrual of sudden privilege, had not diminished in the least. Yet only I had survived the war, and what was I but this opiate, forlorn figure slithering in between the sheets, watching the rain fall unabated on the world, now hard like a barrage from heaven and now gently in bands of mist trailing over treetops, thinking of the dead.

The three slain, and one of them not even in the war, but during the brief armistice that resulted from the younger of the two enemy princes being mortally wounded by our arrows. This brave warrior, my friend the foot soldier, who had given battle fearlessly while managing to save himself from the enemy's blows for so many days, dead with a long knife in his navel, half the blade shining up from the naked flesh, in a room above the tavern, back in the safety of the city's walls, a place to which he had come running the moment the fighting was suspended to slake his passion for a crotchety barmaid, who on the night in question clearly surpassed herself. Murdered out of petty jealousy or anger or some arcane impulse by the most unsuspecting of agents, the same one you can see standing at the side of the cot, hands red with blood and heart madly pounding and white with shame at what she has accomplished without ever intending to. Fortunately for her, she would go unpunished, for the custodians of king's peace are busy elsewhere, looking out, facing an enemy more formidable than a trembling woman beaten by her own crime. One dead and the other constrained to flee, both victims of drives neither could have fathomed in full.

Another killed in action toward the end of battle. Thrown off his horse in the thick of bleeding and warring bodies, and swiftly dispatched to his end by three spears fixing him to the earth at once.

And the third, whom I loved best, the poet, the soldier in front ranks, the maker of charming verses, a rarity, a warrior and a poet, a poet warrior, dead on the first day, all poetry gone out of him. Just at the moment the battle was over. Clubbed to death by that general who some said was a god whose name was Anjaneya. That spy who had entered the palace before the war and had managed to escape after being arrested. But what would it have mattered, this day or the next. On foot, death would have caught up with him one way or another. But on the first day itself, and that too when the battle was over. In stark contravention of the rules of war. A barbaric act. Immoral. Unforgivable. To first rein in the chaos and to then snap the reins yourself. Lay down rules of conduct, cast your net far and wide, and then smartly evade it to satisfy your lust for blood.

My eye was on him as the fighting drew to a close. It was then that I saw the general or the spy or the god coming straight at my friend, who had just a moment ago freed himself from his adversary, disposing of the latter in a hand-to-hand fight, first giving him a clip behind the knee that made his legs cave in and, while his body was helplessly sinking to the ground, fastening his fingers in the victim's nose and breaking his neck with the bottom of a fist, vertebrae and all, extreme work from which my friend was still reeling, when the general yelled at him, demanding engagement. Something like a foreboding, something like a stab of pain, went through my chest and, snatching my mace from its hold, I leapt out of my seat on the elephant's back. I was still on his head, balancing my bulk to run down the trunk and jump into the fray, when the conch shells began to blow, and my sprint was arrested in mid air, hesitation crept round my legs for I felt he was safe now. But not for the attacker, who could simply not control himself, and packed my friend's death in the melancholy moans of the conches, even when he had seen my friend drop his weapon in response to the call for the close of battle.

But once we were alive and together. Often after a long day of suffering the useless etiquette and tiresome verbiage of the courtiers, when my heart would yearn for the rustic music of the street, the sounds and rhythms of my past, for one never outgrows the language of one's youth, I would find them at one or another tavern, lying in drink or rollicking with laughter, or tugging at the soiled skirts and sarongs of the waitresses flitting between the tables, delaying them from their work a moment to flirt or to coo in their ears, lifting the smooth, opaline earlobes on their tongues, or simply rolling dice with other habitual drinkers and degenerates in a corner under a weakly burning oil lamp. After the extreme richness and the clean, soft redolence of the palace, the spirit fumes and the smells of food, tobacco, opium, and bodies so close together made the air in the tavern strangely liberating.

Not that this was the only distinguishing factor between my two haunts. It struck me sometimes, wanderer in different worlds, how unalike were the thoughts and talk of people in the two places. Here, there was no trace of the issues that troubled the great minds at court, the unapologetic strategies and politics of domination and aggression, whether inside the kingdom or beyond its frontiers, the prevailing social and economic conditions, the levy and timely collection of dues, the maintenance of order, suppression of dissent. Not here the sublime talk on art and dialectics, not here the perennial indulgence in silks, jewels, exotic artefacts, not here the elocution, not here the mindless hedonism, unless the term could be applied to men and women living through their labour and instincts alone, speaking fast and without much care, simply to communicate with no desire to impress, full of varying, intense passions in the throes of life. When I thought along these lines, I saw not two worlds but many, an infinite series of mutually exclusive, heterogeneous groups, neither arising from nor influencing each other. Or only minimally. Of this the priests in their liturgies and thinkers in their towers, moneylenders in their tills and sculptors in their stones, monarchs in their dreams of conquest and queens in their unending games and diversions were all equally guilty. Even their tongues bore little resemblance to each other, already specialist jargon was deforming and alienating them, some more than others. Each busy contributing to the whole or divining its ways according to their own peculiar biases and none influencing anything in the end. Sometimes it felt that life moved on not because of, but in spite of our efforts and dealings. Whereas the same day dawned on all, it didn't end the same for everyone. We were a tissue of sentiments that couldn't be reconciled, an ongoing tussle of contrasting, bewildering values, of beauty, knowledge, speculation, ethics, commingling, separating, combining anew, rising willy-nilly above a sea of violent drives like whales coming up to draw breath. Meaning certainly could be had in this, but meaning itself could not be found.

In war alone, then, there seemed a common ground. Here, at least, the enemy had been set apart, given shape and size, a corporeality that could be ruined, here, on the battlefield, was the longed for meeting point of our disparate positions and biases. Was this truly the reason why wars were waged?

One evening I found the poet drinking with two foreign sailors, who had a smattering of our tongue and were telling of their fascination with the gold in our city, how even the mud huts had streaks of gold in them, interspersing this with their adventures on distant coasts and among strange tribes, the aggressive nature of our women, the majesty of our ports, the high export tariffs on certain herbs and spices, the strength of our ale that brought on bouts of homesickness. On and on went the baritone voices, rising from a level deeper in the chest than usual, attesting to their otherness, to each speech its own home in the heart. My friend went along nodding his head, half-listening, half-smiling, bent on scratching words over the heavily indented and marked wood of the table at the end of the patio. Above them the lamp flickered and swayed in the wind that went sighing along the wall, surrounding them lay the dark awash with stars. The other two of our group were away with their regiments. I slipped beside him wordlessly on the bench, and tried to make out the script that was being written over or perhaps re-writing the remains of those that had gone before, etchings emptied of all meaning, or simply empty etchings, made for no reason but to keep the hand and the mind employed while one waited for company or thought one's deepest thoughts. I could see nothing. The words lay dissolved in that age-old palimpsest of wood. I looked at him, and he moved his lips to my ears, breathing the words slowly into them, with a weight that aroused wonder, and at once I saw rising from the chaos of scratches four spidery forms of perfect beauty. The words, the wonder, distilling something from nothing, consciousness entering matter.

Sometime during the night the rain had stopped. As suddenly as they had built up, the clouds faded away and the moon shone in a vast halo over a silent world. The silence pushed me further down into sleep, and I did not awake until late the next day. For several days I had not stepped out of the building and, used to this inner migration, I lingered inside and on the landing for a long time before climbing down the steps to the still wet earth. I retraced the path I had come by for a while, and then took a branch that went along a swale and up into another ridge. Countless rivulets ran down the forest floor into valleys hidden from sight. In the distance, lone white columns of smoke rose obliquely from the wet green hills. More travellers?, more hermits? How had they survived the deluge? The road was still soft, and in places mud reached up to my ankles. The sun lay low on the horizon, the breeze cool and smelling of earth and leaf. Suddenly, there came in view a gigantic iron bell in a rotting wood shelter, open to the four winds, high up at the end of the path. Solid and heavy, a ton or two in weight, it was the last remaining relic of the lost age, its purpose and splendour now forgotten and irrecoverable, the work of gods or giants or beings from beyond. Who else could have put it up here? Behind it at some distance a tree had been caught in the evening's receding light, its leaves grading from silver to pink under the gloss. Black and heavy and imperishable, the bell reflected no light. Its gong, if it could have been moved by a human hand, would have sounded for miles. At the centre of a fluid, unstable universe, this was the one incorruptible object. A moon-moth, lighter than a feather, sat still on its dark curving bulk, creating a contrast inhuman in its beauty. Just then a crow broke into a harsh trailing caw, which went through the setting like a shard of glass goes through flesh. But maybe the simile will not hold. Or only partly.

The shining tree, the bell and the moth, the dry, lingering karking of the bird, to connect them and hold them in the depth of my heart, to squeeze out from them every last drop of happiness, was this, then, my sole reason for living?

XI

SEE THE hand that moves the piece? There is no hesitation in it. Not even premeditation. Only the faint beginnings of pleasure or something resembling it, even if the player is yet to feel it, or cannot locate its source or reason. It is that something unexplained we experience from directing another's pursuits or at least when we believe we are doing so, conveniently forgetting, while our gaze is trained elsewhere, that this pleasure is not for us alone.

Yet because they are simple wood or ivory pieces, dependent on the players' mercy for their movement, and because the players are closeted high up in their terrace gardens away from the press of human wills or history, the fiction, for the time being at least, is sustained. In fact, what neither of the players in this instance has noticed, so profound have been the changes wrought in this respect, so recent their altered positions that we may easily condone the ignorance on their part, is that the pleasure welling up in them is in truth a pleasure which stems not from the freedom to move but from the freedom to exercise control.

Why was the dice abandoned? For one reason alone. That fate ruled the board as it ruled us. That in every throw of the dice was unleashed on us afresh the remembrance of how properly and utterly we were tied in to its designs. Removing the dice from the game's functioning created the twin fiction of our freedom from forces we little understood, and our sole dominion over these tiny actors in the square field of our scrutiny. Go forth and vanquish the foe however you desire, spoke the new voice. This transference of will, or the illusion of its transference, is the game's special lure, this its ultimate evil. So it is that loss and win are felt more profoundly than in any other game, for seldom can the illusion of will seem so smoothly manifest. Ask yourself why you so gladly measure your days and nights in the squares that reflect them? For the pleasure of lifting the tiny weight away from the smooth floor of the board to place it where you and only you wish it to be.

When Misa, stirring from her inertia, heeded the queen's words and, hovering her fingers over her army, still undecided, suddenly pushed the pawn one square forward from the horse on the king's flank, she did so unthinkingly, as if the dice still dictated movement. Reason and will had not yet begun to operate in her, had not had time enough to evict fate from the board, for time certainly is needed before thought may engender total illusion. What this move achieved though was to open the diagonal for the ship's advance. A better move at least than shifting the ship's or the elephant's pawn, which would have freed no channel for either of the larger pieces, given that the horse could have performed its oblique jump anyway.

But no matter how unthinking the first move, choices had begun to grow. On her part, the queen did not take long to respond. Neither was she distracted. She took the one step which was crucial even in the old game. To take hold of one or more of the centre squares on the board. And so she pushed the king's pawn a square forward. Misa could hardly wait to think now, the pieces had started to cast their pull on her, one controls but is controlled in the process. Paying no attention to her adversary's actions, she quickly picked up the second of the horse's pawns, this time on the queen's flank, and repeated her previous move.

For a while they continued in this manner, the queen fortifying her attack in the middle, and Misa building the pressure from the sides, until it looked as if the black forces were being swallowed up by the yellow battalion. Although it did not occur to her at first, somewhere in the back of her mind, the queen had the idea to advance herself, that is to say, the piece newly rendered in her image, as soon as possible. But because the piece was tied to the king, could only slide a single square diagonally around him, and because the king could not move or be brought into the action just yet, to risk so much simply to further one's ambition would be sheer folly, she was beginning to feel annoyed as she moved her ships and horses, her pawns and elephants, without any real strategy though with foresight enough to avoid any unnecessary sacrifices, to challenge Misa's fast spreading army.

Eyes on the board, rarely meeting their rival's, hands, one just slightly longer than the other, lifting dark or pale pieces by turn and depositing them here and there, changing the relation of every piece to every other at every step, attacking and retreating and then attacking anew, creating countless geometric shapes and angles, one upon another, one in another, one beside another, triangles, rectangles, squares, polygons, parallel lines, intersecting lines, every design conceivable in our imagined geometry of spaces except the most imaginary and elusive of all, the circle, hollowing out from one edge only to crowd in a second, black and yellow pieces sliding past each other, occluding each other, capturing each other, free, able, ferocious.

The first exchange took place after some ten or twelve seemingly harmless moves. Misa took a pawn with a horse, and it made her almost weak with joy. But the queen hardly noticed. All her energies were concentrated on advancing into the fray, and soon she was dragging the king along all over the board, flouting with impunity the most basic of rules. The second exchange, if exchange it was and not carnage, removed seven pieces one after another from the board, and not even then did the players stop to think.

By now the game had taken away any remaining sense of judgment. Empty pools, voids really, formed and dissolved, like notes in a fervent composition, in the four corners of the board, but the players rushed on, wholly consumed by the momentum of the game, the fire of its possibilities, consolidating their respective forces, eager to launch a second offensive, waging their swift silent battle on a narrow strip of wood.

Thrice it happened that Misa confused the correct square to which a piece could be moved. The squares all blank, the rules so new, the hunger so urgent, the thrill so palpable, she misplaced the diagonal along which the ship could be shifted more than once. Another time the horse landed a square short in its angular leap. Once, too, the queen moved herself away from the king by more than a square, and promptly catching her mistake, Misa, excited, intervened. That is wrong. You cannot venture that far from the king. And the queen, feeling the sudden pull of chains on her flesh, retreated, dismayed by her impotence, the net of rules cut through only to be now caught back in its sweeping tails.

Some more of this ludic display, some more pieces scattered along the perimeter of the board, some more reconfiguration of forces, and for the first time the players start to think ahead, to loosely strategize. The endgame had begun.

The enemy king had come out from behind the ranks of his warriors, and the queen's sole wish was to slay him with her beloved piece alone, and to this end she began to plot moves, push her king and pawns here and there to clear the way for her own dawdling advance, patiently sliding behind or along with them but getting nowhere, destined, alas, to lamely orbit the king forever, tied to the greater piece, but why?, like a planet to a star.

The queen won the first game. But she felt no happiness as she moved the elephant from the end of the board where it had lain from the very beginning of play to eject the enemy king off its square. Yet another oversight of Misa's had presented her with an opportunity too good to be passed over, and in the end feasibility won over wishfulness. The elephant's path though long was clear, and the queen was so close yet so far. Such was her preoccupation with her thoughts, such her disheartenment with the rules she had herself not long ago prescribed that she did not see the shame of loss in Misa's eyes, something she had not seen before in that most loving and gentle girl. Thus it happened that both players came away more unhappy than before from their first engagement.

But the wind went about unheeded, so did the peacocks in the lawns, so the water in the fountains, so the sun in the sky, unusually mild on this day for the tropics. So much has transpired in so short a time, but to the ladies-in-waiting it means nothing. They have not seen anything out of the ordinary except two bored members of royalty amusing themselves at yet another game, dice or no dice, four or two teams, it is all the same to them. They have not seen anything, for they have not been shown. They have not been made to see.

XII

NIGHT AND day the coitus continues. The bodies coil and uncoil, merge and detach in such a variety of forms that you wonder if they are one, two, or many, forever delaying the moment of climax like in a long, digressive novel. But if the climax is not delayed then the pleasure is not prolonged, desire perishes in a fleeting if charming release. Pleasure needs time just as time needs pleasure to fuse and explode into emptiness, thus freed from each other's bondage, they leave no residue, active or dead matter.

But let us return to the conjugal scene, where there is no desire, or rather into which desire has not yet made its appearance or where it exists but is not felt. Strange as it may seem, the concupiscence which is commonly the supreme driver of bodily pleasure is totally absent from this carnal rite, if carnal at all it is and not ethereal, for as we well know appearances are often deceptive.

King and queen, husband and wife, the yogin and his consort, the goddess Tara, Śiva as Bhairava, the Fearful Lord, and Śakti as Bhairavi, the Fearful Goddess, each form collapsing into the next as impressions passing and breaking over the lake of flesh. The many-limbed, many-gestured, interminable tantric dance.

The man firm like a rock or a mountain or a tree, unwavering, unexcitable, a mind empty of all desire, the woman serene, pliant, munificent, committed to give and receive without distrust, the two enacting, in the very image of a vine clasping a tree, the *Śiva Lata Mudra*.

Here the wish for pleasure does not lead to forgetfulness, to lose oneself in the aspect of the other, but instead to fierce control and concentration, an intense self-identification with the life-force surging within. For three, five, eight hours, the couple sit face to face in the royal bed, without a shred of clothing, without the least excitation, until each has achieved complete one-pointedness of mind, at which time there is felt at the base of the spine, as if just born, a granule of heat. They have no consciousness of time, no vision of day or night, neither hunger nor thirst.

Next, the king moves the queen onto his left thigh, eyes locked into each other, sexes close but not touching, they sit in perfect equanimity for several hours.

Still on his lap, the queen is now facing forward, their figures erect, his left arm curving behind her back to gently cup the left breast, while her right arm drapes into his lap, hand lightly entwining the erection. Already it is night, the flames dim, moonshine filling the room, stars few but hard and glittering like diamonds. By the time they finally join, dusk is again falling, but the very act of coitus is far from begun. It is yet another pose, yet another level of descent, and the seed the king has held within him for all those years and months of roving through the harsh, cold, rim of the earth will spurt not yet.

They are both familiar with the ancient, venerable technique of sucking up water through their sexual orifices by a certain way of breathing or to be precise by stopping the breath altogether at specific places in the body. But water, in what the king is now proposing, is merely the first of a further row of steps, a cleansing agent to prepare the vessel of the body for receiving the terrible inhuman love, if love it be, by which the universe is made.

When water has cleansed and been expelled, it is the turn of milk to be taken in and held up for a few hours, to cool the glands and pave the way for what will come hence. Like water, so with milk. Likewise clarified butter. Each element denser than the one before, each held for longer, building patience and reserve in the bearers, testing stamina, for the act to which they are progressing will brook no weakness, yield to no emotion.

The couple have perfected their systems, are utterly indifferent to the heaviness in their perineums. Now comes the last step, the supreme test of the bodies to be able to withstand what is to follow, a rite of the adepts. It is then that the king brings out a small container from which he pours two or three spoonfuls of purified quicksilver into a shallow dish. Mercury, that strangest of metals, element of the gods, catalyst of transmutation. Heavy in its fluidity, protean in its sturdiness. Like how the mind is, or ought to be. For the first time, as the metal is breathed in, globes of sweat appear on their skins, one pale, the other coppery. The granule of heat born at the bottom of the spine has set the solar plexus alight. Soon the blazing fire is sent slithering by this fierce agent to every extremity of the body, heat is spreading in widening circles, temperatures are on the rise, feet and the mind baking alike in the kiln of flesh. Desire possesses them completely without their in the least possessing it. The edge of the world as also its navel as also the seed from which it sprouted into being, the square brick altar as also the sacred fire kindling within as also the sacrificial or symbolic offerings poured into it, so many signs winding into each other to make up the touching, desiring bodies.

A thousand sighs, a hundred peakings with just the king's fingers on the frets of the queen's flesh that glint here and there in her skin as light from the moon shifts across her body. On and on he plays her like a *vīnā*, her music streaming in a delicate symphony of sounds, *ragas* that know no crescendo, no culmination.

At last the vulva surrounds the phallus, engulfs it. Like dark space engulfing matter, like a lake possessing a mountain's image, like night covering the gloss of the world. Like a wedge his torso locks into her wet angular thighs.

Conjoined, moist, glistening bodies that have become their own altars, their own pious mandalas with tiers descending one inside the other, home to all peaceful and wrathful deities dancing in the concentric arcs of the mind, pointing within at the pure land, a blue luminous tiny square space in the heart of which shines the *Vajra*, the indestructible, all destroying mace of Indra, which is also the thunderbolt which is also the forever glittering diamond of bliss and emptiness and oneness. Symbols here are useless, loosening away from the thing itself, they show their infirmity, reflecting and cancelling out one another in their own hall of mirrors. Device, word, knowledge finally merge together on this, the third night of the supreme coitus, to help the participants riding the wheel of great bliss, *Cakrasamvara*, to transcend the wheel of time, *Kālacakra*, itself.

When they separate, when a new dawn breaks, when the king leaves the queen's bed, the two have exhausted the entire spectrum of desire within themselves. Never will they come together again like this, never will the flame of longing flicker in the body of one for the other with such intensity. But is it desire alone that has been exhausted? Or memories too? If not completely, then in some measure the past has begun to disintegrate. A slight gap has opened that will widen and be filled anew. Different passions will arise and grow and in time repaint the mind's canvas, for life itself has not ceased yet. Whereas the queen will be pulled by the board's lure, the magic of its shifting currents, the king will put his strange liquid metal to new, unbelievable uses, most significantly to the prototype of the flying machine lying discarded in some corner shed of the palace.

At present it is nothing but a wooden hemispherical shell big enough to seat four, encrusted, round its edge, in jewels possessing properties that react to the elements in varying ways, decorated with the head and wings of the mythic bird *haṃsa*, part swan, part goose, with three closed vessels containing gyroscopes, placed at specific points in the hull. Mythic, surely, but dead too. Nothing but wood, alloy, cloth, and jewel. What it needs to take flight is a force, a consciousness, which the king will before long implant in its breast. Not for nothing has he learnt the various characteristics and functions of mercury, which he carries with him wherever he goes.

He knows how to bend it to his will, to his own subtle energies, and more than that, he knows that it can conduct the incredible power of the thunderbolt to create a force field. All he need do is to make the liquid run in a channel around the gyroscope and through a few conducting wires transfer the charge in the higher reaches of the atmosphere into the vessels. The rest he will manage simply by directing its course through concentration of thought. He will ride the bird, and like the earth so in the sky will he reign.

Life moving in circles. Better still, life moving in cycles. Learning, unlearning, learning afresh. To purge pride utterly inside oneself, only to find it streaming in from a chink so soon. From there what a short way it is to rage, to madness, to destruction. The weakening of the organism to let the parasite of evil action, from lives past or present, enter and defile the host yet again.

XIII

MUSIC, OPENING wide the portals of thought, slackening the bonds of flesh on the spirit, turning the water in jars sweeter by degrees.

Tall and heavy, his thinning hair falling in curls over his neck, a zither on his lap, the maestro sings into the cool tropical night to the accompaniment of a four-piece musical ensemble. Lamps burning in glass shades along the dais, and the walls of the courtyard filled with an ink-black air whose edges are swamped with stars. Gestures, modulations, faint unnoticed blinks to the prevailing deities of the night. The swish of an arm catching a note in the air, not just the chords in the throat, but the whole body performing and shuddering to the music, a great river of music flowing through and flooding the banks. A few lines of verse, ten or twelve words, not more, charged with ancient meaning or wisdom, sometimes merely expressing an aphorism or a yearning, sung a thousand times over in shifting patterns of notes with ever changing intervals, rhythms, improvisations, here performing a swift short glide through words or suddenly breaking them into their constituent syllables which come whole again miraculously to make up an octave, there rising and falling and oscillating in notes, rolling in echoes, and at last breaking into a majestic howl, enacting the possibilities of speech to its very end, and then even beyond that end, catenated molecules of sound dissolving into soft strands of breath, and breath vanishing into silence or music of a kind the ear cannot yet detect whereby the auditor's soul takes flight with the dying vocals to travel and spread across the empyrean, and there is every fear of it not returning.

The voice returns to earth and brings back with it the queen's soul and her heart begins to beat again. This kind of dislocation of thought she has not felt in years. When last was the mind so emptied out? When was it the king held her in that unending embrace?

An entire month has elapsed since that first fateful encounter over the board. Fateful not because of the results of the match, which, if anything, had been all but forgotten by the same evening, but because what took place over the board had been so altered as to bewitch any interested mind with a single glance. That is, for a mind in the know of the old game, of how a spectacular effect was achieved by a simple rearrangement of its component elements. How much more should the bewitchment be then for her who engendered it? Bewitchment that was also enervating and irksome. The case of all creators who take their task passionately and in earnest. Where others see a smooth synthesis of beauty and wit, the creator finds only torn and hanging sinews, architectonic problems, concerns over pace and rhythm, obfuscation. In brief, she knows too much about the game's defects to take heart from its striking achievements. This though is just an early version, at best a pointer to where the game can go, what it can become.

The first and the most pressing, perhaps the only, problem is the pace of the game. Or rather the pace or sweep of certain pieces. Better still the sweep of one piece in particular, the Queen. Why, she has asked herself countless times in the past days, is she bound to move about the king, as if still in chains?

The very next day, upon devising the new mode of play, the queen had called for the master carver and instructed him to make for her two complete sets of pieces, one of ebony and the other of ivory, with small, varying, leaden weights buried in each piece's base, such that wood weighed as much as ivory, king as much as king, pawn equivalent to pawn, and horses likewise, each piece just heavy enough to rouse the mind of the player who lifted it. Alongside this she described how certain pieces had to be remodelled, how the chariot had to be carved in the image of a boat, complete with its mast and sails, and the Queen in the image of the King, save for the crown, a replacement for which she drew on the spot for the carver's benefit as a perfect replica of her own diadem.

Now that the few physical departures in the new game had been dealt with, the more abstract of its aspects besieged her. But at this point all inspiration deserted, and she moved the pieces this way and that, testing the feasibility of fresh moves in the larger scheme of the game itself, which, however, and this was crucial, would preserve its delicate equilibrium. Yet she could not bring herself to it, nor saw any way of doing this. To her the moves were perfect, could not be bettered, each one following a different trajectory that contrasted and complemented all others to make up the unique multi-layered texture of the game. And yet she knew something was amiss, something *could* be improved. For as long as the Queen was not set free, she could well turn back to the old ludo and be done with the whole sorry matter for good. Howsoever more advanced than its precursor it was, this game of hers still fell short of giving her the joy she had half-knowingly envisaged.

To the one who perseveres not every solution occurs with equal ease, or indeed occurs at all. That said, one must keep searching, open and patient, holding doubt at bay, looking for the spark that, if the angle be right, is released from one thing's coming in contact with another. What else is beauty or inspiration of which the poets sing, if not the roving gaze suddenly held still upon the chance meeting of two or more objects, a small silk-and-bamboo fan resting against a glass jar, say, and drawing out from this combination their deepest essence. An essence not in the object but in the gaze narrowing into focus amid the chaotic bounty of the world. To each wandering gaze, its own essence.

In five days, the recast pieces were delivered to her, and as she admiringly placed them over the board, she saw something she hadn't previously seen. Because the chariot, now a compact, stream-lined ship, moved diagonally over the squares, was it not better perhaps to bring it up-close to the royal pair, such that it may possess not one but two diagonals from the start and not be left stranded at the very edge of the board? Instantly, the elephant and the ship exchanged their respective positions round the horse on either flank, and just as this was done, there arose in her the idea, perchance out of proximity, that she may at least give the Queen the ship's powers, such that she could move two squares diagonally in either direction as against the earlier move of a single square.

Another ten days passed, but she did not cease to think, indeed her mind raced through several permutations one after the other. The root of her trouble, she believed, was primarily aesthetic, though behind it lurked a certain ambition as well. Prior to this latest modification, each type had its unique movement, but now all she had done was to give to the board another chariot or ship with the airs of a Regina. No, she was no mere charioteer or shipmaster. What was to be done though? Going back was unthinkable. But what new move could be added to her repertoire? How to rise above these ships and horses and footmen and not be merely their equal? The King may watch from behind the ranks, move with his slow, cautious tread in a guarded territory, but she would not wait by his side like a mute spectator or a dainty consort, she would boldly push forth into combat at whatever cost, even command the entire army if need be.

Outwardly calm but seething with turmoil underneath, she went through the days without once bringing up with Misa the subject of the game or the prospect of a rematch, even avoiding her at times, fearing a hint or, what was worse, a challenge from this former opponent waiting to avenge a past defeat. To play again before she had resolved her predicament would be agony. No, not till I have perfected the rules, the queen reasoned with herself. Thus, day after day she went about moving pieces in her head or, in the quiet privacy of her rooms, over the board itself.

By the month's end she had conveniently appropriated some of the elephant's powers too. Now she could move two squares in any direction on the board. This was cause for relief. Each type had its own special gait once more, the harmony and variety of the game restored. The shackles at last had come undone.

Late in the night of the musical performance the queen fell into a liminal state. The pleasure that had been denied her all this while at last entered her, and the next day she was ready to play. But she did not call for the girl till late evening, and when the meeting did take place, it was Misa instead who enquired whether they should not play another game the following morning. In her own chambers, she had been privately poring over the board all through this time, seemingly playing with herself, but in fact just enjoying the physical proximity of the board and the pieces, for without the dice they had suddenly become living, palpable entities. Taking her cue from the queen, she had arranged two full sets of forces on either end of the board, first by calling for an entire spare set and fishing out from the velvet-lined case black and yellow pieces that lay jumbled up with green and red of their kind, and then by partly slicing off the crowns of the two additional kings to fashion the respective queens. The urge to play a real game, however, soon developed in her, and at the month's end she burst forth into the queen's chambers asking her to a match.

Back at their previous spot in the terrace gardens the ensuing day, indifferent to the strutting peacocks opening their tails in a shining blue-green fan, indifferent too to the ornate symmetry of the gardens, the turning drip of the fountains falling in coloured pools, the warm beams of the sun and the cool breeze of the sea, the half-full lightly steaming teacups, unaware of the many attendants unknowingly replicating around them the very angles formed by the patches of perfectly mowed lawns just as the attendants were unaware of everything except the bids and gestures of these royal personages, the queen began placing the new pieces on the board beneath the excited gaze of the girl.

When Misa had lifted and admired each and every piece, when she had made the queen promise to get a spare set of perfect replicas cast for her, when the queen had shown and explained the fresh changes in arrangement and powers that she had dreamt up during the past month, among them relaxing rules of capture, for now any piece could take any other, which to the girl was all the same, impatient as she was to begin the game, and when the forces were stationed and ready, each at the centre of its square, restless to advance, play commenced.

Eager to charge onward into the fray, the queen opened her game again with the two centre pawns, easing the passage for her queen, but for the ships too. Misa this time responded with identical steps, and very soon the pawns in the queen file stood blocking each other, backed by their respective seconds in the king file, not unlike duellists approaching and apprehending one another. But there they stayed for the time being, the moment of reckoning deferred. Meanwhile the dark queen came gliding forward abreast of the king's pawn, one after another rival horsemen hopscotched into battle, ships attacked the open diagonals, then the queen again, then another pawn sallying forth. At this point one of the seconds stirred into action, and in a lightning stroke neutralized the rival duellist, a move that would have been impermissible in the outside world was in the board's compact domain only right and reasonable. But the two were under attack in an instant from every quarter, and were wiped out in quick succession, until there survived not a trace of the duel, the patch of ground empty as before, free to be traversed or used for a fresh encounter. Little strategy but unmitigated thirst for action on either side, and play progressing haphazardly though speedily. In just about a few minutes the game's spell was total and relentless, the strain on their nerves building unbeknown to the players. The queen was daring but alert, while Misa, utterly in thrall to the swift ruthless beauty of her ivory pieces, dashed headlong without care and struck without hesitation, not once planning ahead for anything like an endgame, if endgame, that is, could have had even a remote bearing on minds so beguiled by the flow of forces unfolding in a whirlpool of warfare. Deaths on both sides, regardless of station or influence, were on the rise, bigger and bigger gaps were opening and closing in different parts of the field, tilting and turning the game's axis perpetually and unpredictably, yet the speed of engagement did not ease. The tall handsomely carved pieces were delighting Misa so much that she had twice already overreached herself by pushing one of her ships farther than was permitted. But where was the limit of the permissible in a game whose limits were being continually redrawn? The queen although noticing such aberrations, did not once correct her. In truth, it was not so much an overreach as a simple confusion regarding the right square. The cells all plain, the moves so quick, the exchange between emptiness and fullness constant and shifting from square to square, it was not difficult to see why Misa landed in the wrong place now and then. These few innocuous moves on her part, however, made her adversary ever bolder and she, this adversary, now reasoned with herself why the queen couldn't do what the ship was so easily doing. In the very next move, therefore, she advanced the queen far out into the enemy's left flank and slew the elephant which was only now beginning to take a more active role in the game. Thinking herself gone too far, past all limits, yet not wishing to retract, the queen trembled inwardly from a strange mix of thrill and anxiety, an anxious thrill or a thrilling anxiety. But rather than objecting to this patently false move, Misa gauged the situation astutely and responded likewise. The next instant a horseman lay dead on the very square he had so gallantly wrested from an enemy soldier. Like a symphony, like a painting, like a poem in the act of being composed, the game by now had developed its own wisdom and was issuing forth undaunted, drawing fresh breath on each step, stretching its own material to make space for yet more creativity, bearing along the happy and astonished pair into newer, unseen realms.

Even though the queen lost this time, she was hardly displeased. For here was everything she had once wished for. Speed, agility, daring. What with the dice would have taken at least half a day to finish, now could be accomplished inside of an hour, maybe even faster. Sufficient encouragement then to take matters in your hands, and to rid yourself forever of such double-faced notions as chance, destiny, fatalism. The mind alone was real, the will in itself everything.

But here one was already skirting the solipsistic abyss. Whose mind, whose will, you would ask? Weren't there already two wills clashing over the board, two minds begetting their own distinct realities? Was not chance already at play, if it had ever vanished?

Of all the achievements, of all the inventions, the queen bestowed to the erstwhile game, there was one crucial development that did not come from her. The chequered pattern of the board. Beset with general confusion as the play progressed and to ease their memory of the forever changing positions of the pieces, many a player had even in the older game adopted chequered boards to their great relief and advantage, a pattern both overfamiliar and archetypal, stamped in our psyche by the eternal roll of nights and days, by the shadow at our feet, by the subtle gradations of form in a colourless void, by our innate love of, indeed our inability to do without contrast. Boards such that they, our players, themselves had seen in the past but not made much of, boards that were now indispensable aids for the complex moves and wide sweeps of the game, boards that at once helped the game and added yet more symmetry, more nuance to its design. Two teams, two colours, as above so as below.

And yet where would her ambition be, had the thought come to the queen before the match? For it is sometimes better to err, to overlook slight faults in others than to bring them to task and never yourself stray from the open road. Sometimes it is better to discover only belatedly.

The cold untouched teacups have been replaced with fresh ones. Amid these carefully ordered lawns, the shuffling peacocks fluting in the wind, the tenuous spray of fountains and snaky banners humming like sails from bastions and rooftops, and surrounded by attendants silent as phantoms, the players sit quiet and content over the empty wooden board, relishing their drink in a speechless communion.

XIV

BY AND BY the serpentine of the army reached the horn of the
southern peninsula. From here a chain of islets issued out into the
sea to eventually merge with the sprawling archipelago that held in
its cradle the vast kingdom of the demon king to which we were
bound. From the top of the bluff where we stood at the head of the
troops sloping down behind us straight into the jungle, you could
not have known where the grey of the beach ended and the china
blue of the sea began, where a patch of land rose above water and
where it lay a few feet beneath the swells. In truth, there existed an
unbroken, if treacherous, passage up to enemy borderlands across
sandbanks and limestone shoals rich in pearly shells which could be
fished out in fistfuls wherever you dug under water, or came stuck
in the cavities of your toes every few steps. Opalescent clouds
drifted in slow groups toward a burning sun, and dark specks arced
in the sky that were suddenly vultures cutting huge swoops on the
air to attack their prey, while far beyond a half-moon like an
inverted boat calmly sailed in the blue ether. The glare of the sun,
the heat, the humidity after the cool of the forest would have been
stifling were it not for the gusts of wind that rose from the ocean
every now and then and lashed the sweat clean off our skins. I had
travelled far up north, I had gone east and west, but not once had I
come south. This when I had lived all my life hardly a few hundred
miles inland. And now south it was that awaited us. The south. So
calm and enchanting, with not a whiff of the sinister about it. The
sense of the sinister came not from beyond but from behind, from

the unceasing murmurs of our men, from the rumours relating the demonic, preternatural powers of the enemy spreading through the ranks like a plague.

We had come upon lately the news of the demon king flying away with his abductee in a strange craft shaped like a gigantic bird that none could have envisioned in his wildest dreams. And what we cannot envision, we fear. Although the king's influence was not unknown on our earth, he had not waged a campaign against any kingdom on the peninsula in several years, and had been even then mostly content to leave the control of occupied territories in the hands of those he had defeated, simply adopting them as his vassals and receiving an annual tribute in return for his generosity. Great and powerful though he was, that was not the real cause of worry to our soldiers. It was the airship, and the other nameless armaments and contrivances, past our strangest fancies, which would come in its wake.

But the two princes, god-incarnates that they were, observed the vista with admirable sangfroid, eyes clear, brows clean. So did I, the third in line. My friend, however, the chief of the tribe who had barely had the time to enjoy his chiefdom, looked askance, now at the sea and now at one or another of us, in pitch with the thoughts of his men and worried about the morale of the army in general.

Could our information be right? Could the word we had received be trusted? Was it wise to lead the troops into the enemy heartland without first confirming the details of the story?

Before long it was decided that at first I alone would make a covert journey to the island, and see with my own eyes if indeed the princess was held captive in the demon king's palace, and, if so, to reach her without attracting notice and assure her that rescue was near. Part of the plan was also to find the least perilous way to transfer our men across the sea so that they did not suffer great harm and could be ready for battle at short notice. Thus while the rest of the company descended the bluff to bivouac into the forest, I ventured forth toward the beach and thence toward the south where

XIV

I had never been.

From the start, it was not as easy as it looked. True, the water was not deep enough to cause any great trouble, but here and there were strange whirlpools that sucked you in if as much as your shadow fell over them, for by this time you were already unwittingly caught in their current. Alas, no enchantress lying in wait underneath with mouth wide open to swallow you whole whom you may have slain in a contest worthy to be sung in a legend.

The first of the islets were bare and uninhabited with not a rill, not a pond or an abandoned well in the crags and rocks to quench one's thirst. Here, rain fell on the stony landscape and quickly drained out into the sea. Maybe there were to be found swales or hollows in rocks where water had collected, but I was no dowser prospecting for hidden springs, bound as I was on a swift delicate mission, obliged to cut the shortest path to my destination. Yet I did not fail to make a note of this, for lacking enough to drink, the majority of our men would have perished of thirst without once sighting the enemy.

Pale brown landscape and dark blue-grey water alternating for miles on end like a secret pattern wrought in wood. Wading through the sea, then soil and rock beneath the feet, then back into water creaming with salt, undrinkable. Then more patches of dry, sandy, rocky land, with next to no trees or wildlife. Then the sea again, by now turquoise and teeming with life such as I had never seen before, pink and yellow and electric-blue fish, molluscs, corals, and periwinkles.

At last I came upon an isle which appeared noticeably green, the beginning of shrubs and short prickly trees, foxes pricking their ears in a tussock of grass. Soon I found a waterhole and, falling to my knees, lapped up the water greedily in company of crows and herons crowding around its bank or perched on serrated boulders. After the sunset, the temperature dropped and the wind came in fierce howls. But I kept moving. What was here to hold one back? To hunt for a cave in the rocks and light a fire seemed a pointless task.

Without knowing it, I had been for some time skirting the border of the enemy lands. Suddenly, in the distance, I saw clusters of huts surrounded by fields and orchards, mud paths through the fallows and into the trees. And then more fields, more trees, more hills, until I reached the cliff face rising over the forest, affording a most spectacular view of my destination, the seat of the demon king's empire.

It was a bewitching sight, so the child told the puma, for once all beings spoke a common tongue, a speech through which sound and light passed together. Twinkling blue, green, red, and golden lamps rising in tiers from escarpments of buildings and premises up to the royal citadels, outstripping the beauty of the dense starry night above them. My first sighting of a city, and what a splendour it was. Not the work of men, but of giants, of gods even.

Covered in soot, wrapped in a cloak, I slipped into its streets late at night, a picture in contrast, though there were many not unlike me spilling out in the streets from ill-lit public houses and opium dens. How to find the captive princess? Where to search for her? Everything lay coated in gold, releasing a dull, hazy gleam in the darkness. I noticed that even the most modest of dwellings had palisades wrought in bronze with tips of gold. In time I was able to slip behind the palace walls where I moved under the cover of trees in the gardens that surrounded the majestic colonnades from whose blue shadows countless alert eyes kept watch. Thinking where to begin my search, a low sweet voice came to me from a nearby grove, and I instantly intuited that my search was at an end.

Later, relieved by the successful completion of the task handed to me, and curious to see more of the lives of the city's inhabitants, primarily of the royalty, of which the abducted princess had hinted in our brief, furtive conversation while distractedly nibbling a pear, I jumped the fence into the main palace and, hiding from the sentries, soon reached the upper storeys of the building.

Richness and decadence that could have made one's head spin. Murals and tapestries that contained every design and colour, every myth betokening our common heritage, the roots of our perennial disputes and powers. From the first incest and parricide to the oceanic churning that brought forth not only Indra's elephant, Airavata, and the seven-headed flying horse, Uccaihśravas, he who neighs loudly, he the rumble of heavens, but rare and precious jewels that were also the sun, the moon, and the asteroids gyrating in the celestial vaults, and then the nymphs, and lastly, the ambrosia, the sweet nectar of immortality that made gods and demons drool alike, the very thing for which the parties had in the first instance taken the trouble of raising up from the seas their hidden treasures, like butter from milk.

Room upon room with verses of scriptures bursting forth in song through splashes of paint and pigments, silk curtains billowing from the wind, sandalwood carvings, gold idols of kings and sages and terrible divinities, patterned shades, incense sticks going up in whorls of fragrant smoke. A dizzying profusion of colour, perfumes, goblets, bodies drifting against lamps and lettering, yellow on crimson, feasting and carousing amidst untold magnetic objects. All this charm and opulence, while on the opposite shore countless men waiting to explode out of the forest, cross the sea, and precipitate a crisis in the heart of this endless celebration . . .

In another wing, on the far side of the palace, where rooms were bigger and emptier, I found a woman, the queen?, with her back to the window. I did not chance, in any of the chambers, upon the king, whom I had half-knowingly most wanted to see, but my wish was soon to come true, as all wishes in time do, for the thought itself is the key. So beware of wishing lest what comes in its wake catches you unaware, unprepared, at your wits' end. Wave upon wave of desire breaking against the shore of the world that is also the mind, retreating, collecting, colliding again, forming and reforming its very landscape beyond wish, beyond recognition.

Passing from frame to frame, I suddenly encountered a most fascinating sight, bewitchment of all bewitchments, if bewitchment by then had not lost its meaning, and here to my annoyance I stopped. A man and a woman were bent over a strange kind of activity. A chequered wooden board with what appeared to be two diminutive armies, black and white, mirroring the very pattern of the board, each with its horses, ships, and elephants, waging war upon one another. Were the two simply amusing themselves at an evening game, and what a peculiar game!, or had they by chance got a whiff of our plan to mount an attack, and were devising and testing different strategies of defence and combat? It was unlikely. Why would the man, even if he were high enough in the ranks to decide such things, involve a young woman in formulating battle tactics? What could she know of war? Moreover, our army was mostly on foot, at most a chariot or two, a few horses or elephants, but nothing to equal the meticulous fourfold symmetry of the enemy forces, as seemed to be the case on the board. Intricately beautiful and organic though it looked, there was about it something abstract, something merely artistic. Yet I watched the moves carefully to understand their operation, and soon I was itching to touch and hold the pieces, so handsomely designed, to push and shift them from this to that dark or pale square, picking along the way moves, rules, combina-tions, how certain pieces stood frozen in the vicinity of others, while some pounced upon the enemy the moment they caught sight of him. Lines of threat and safety shifted perpetually and completely at every step. The black at all times looked vulnerable, and looking up from the hand directing it I understood why this was so. The man had only one eye on the game, his attention solely concentrated on his adversary and rarely on her moves. It was clear to me that he was in love, though from his cautious stance and silence, the way his eyes scarcely met the other's or flitted across her person, his slight nervousness plainly visible, it was not difficult to deduce that these were still early times of courtship.

The woman was of a type I had never seen before. Certainly not born on the island, not even on our peninsula, but from someplace else. Skin so pale and smooth, gestures so subtle, a touch so light. Prominent cheekbones that lent a deep stillness to her small black eyes with spots of shine in them, and a most delicate chin and nose, not a pinch of flesh anywhere more than was necessary, even if it was the slight fleshiness in places that gave her face its striking elegance. A slow ache rose in my heart, a feeling not of love, or what passes for love in the world, but of something infinitely higher, heavy without being heavy, at once substantial and light, gathered and fell in my throat like a lump, like a bite of peach I had forgotten to chew. I could well understand why the man had fallen for her. The man unable to search the face of his beloved for long and gladly suffering for it, the woman with eyes only for the game unfolding before her and of which she was in no small part the cause, the game with its symmetry and fluidity, the dance of light, colour, and shadow, the breeze flowing in from the sea, the distant shimmer of stars, and the softly glowing palace walls, triangle upon triangle, held me in a complex, manifold geometry.

Engrossed in this triadic palimpsest, I did not notice that the man had seen me peering from the window, his gaze had wandered, for inattention in one thing is inattention in everything, and had gestured, perhaps by simply slanting his head in my direction, connecting my form to the eyes that were trained to observe and locate their object with a swift ease, to the sentinels who were now sneaking up on me from both sides. I could have made an escape there and then, they would never have been able to lay a hand on me, yet I let them arrest me and parade me into the palace. More than one wish was at work. But the spell had been broken, the wind had died down near the ground, while up above a thin sheet of grey was veiling the stars that suddenly seemed indifferent.

The king was alerted. The man who had so smoothly had me arrested and of whom I would see more in battle, expertly riding and manoeuvring his elephant through the warring masses, waited in a corner with two or three courtiers. Silence hung in the air and shadows crawled along the corners of the impressive ceiling adorned in gold curlicues. To judge from the quiet forms trickling in, news of my capture had spread fast through the palace. With my hands tied behind my back and everyone avoiding my eye, I waited like the rest for the arrival of the king, whose prerogative alone it seemed to interrogate the one who had been captured and detained in the act of spying. Thinking over my situation calmly, it occurred to me that perhaps I could loosely explain my position and persuade or pray to the king to let the captive princess leave with me, and thus avoid the great bloodshed and misery which were otherwise bound to follow. Little more than wishful thinking it was, helping the mind to pass time. Did the king himself know for sure why he had abducted the woman? And why should he trust a spy?

The king came through the east door. There was little curiosity or vexation in those eyes, the only intelligent eyes in the hurriedly convened gathering. From the start, it was not easy to read the man, and I teetered between two opposing strains of feeling, whether to appeal to the king's generosity as I had earlier envisaged, or turn inward, offering nothing, until I was banished to the dungeon or sentenced to the gallows, from where I would escape at the first available opportunity. Despite all previous reasoning, I decided to choose the latter, and stay utterly quiet through any ensuing interrogation, calmly awaiting the sentence to be read out. The king didn't look much interested, nor did he begin at once. One after another, questions were put to me by different voices in the assembly, enraged or impassioned depending on their intensity, to each of which my answer was the same, silence. What could I say to these livid fools merely enacting their long assigned roles to the best of their ability? My position and imagined explanations were unnecessary and ridiculous here. And yet when the king bade me speak, emotion gripped my throat, my innards burned, and I spat words like glowing coals, as if I could hold them inside no longer.

In spite of this, however, I had not yet relinquished control over my thoughts, and the words which I spoke still feared the mind's whip. But it was enough to tell the king what was going on, he may have expected it anyway from the complete lack of surprise the news made on him in contrast to others who appeared grossly outraged as if I had been unfair in my assessment.

The king heard me silently, almost indiffe ntly, not even speaking when I finished or when speech itself ha sunk back into a subterranean stream. But then unexpectedly a piercing laughter rang out, and I felt as if the heavens themselves were coming apart, falling in large shards and with a great force all over me. Evil, I figured, lay not in the depravity of the act, but in the ignorance of its causes.

The king dismissed me with a wave of his arm. Enough of this comedy, I thought. Time to head back. My task was done here. What would follow would follow. I did not know where I was being led, but I complied willingly with my captors' directions, their pushing and shoving, their needless playacting. Finally we arrived at an open space with trees and bushes. Nothing could be better. From a balcony high above, the diminished form of the king watched the proceedings. Here to my surprise they tied a rag dipped in some combustible substance round my waist and put it to flame. This was entirely unnecessary and despite myself anger flared up in me. Just as the sentries drew apart from the ring of fire surrounding my form, I swiftly untied my hands on which I had been at work for some time and taking the burning cloth from one edge, climbed the nearest wall at lightning speed and set alight a whole lot of silks and tapestries.

How quickly the fires spread, with what ease an entire wing went up in flames. And then another. The king had not left his place on the balcony, and when I jumped here and there, giving a slip to the mob of sentinels loosed upon me, I came right where he stood. He made no attempt to catch me, as if he were a bystander with no part to play in what was happening at only an arm's length from him, watching the scene with only marginal interest. When I leaped off into the dark from the last of the crenellations, half the palace burning behind me, I could still see his eyes which had in them an expression not of rage, not of surprise, not even of indifference, but something behind or beyond these feelings, an aura of inevitability that cloaks and fixes what has gone before though seldom that which is to come. Yes, in those eyes, the future appeared at the moment as irrevocable as the past.

XV

NOW THAT I think about the past in my self-imposed solitude, a
ghost among ghosts in this crumbling forest lodge it is difficult to
say when things began to worsen, when love sprouted in my breast
and when it was snatched away by events over which I had little
control, that seemed to happen at a distance, but whose slow, broad
sweep did not fail to upend my life. Today as the past is nothing but
a few sodden tissues of dream that doggedly cling to the mind's
weave, unwilling to let go, I can perhaps surmise that things at times
occur too late for us or rather we arrive at the stage only belatedly,
our interest is kindled at the very last moment, near the finishing
line although the line is not yet visible or has been obliterated by our
belief in the turf's being endless, with many twists and turns, letting
us enter or exit anywhere, forgetting so easily that such is the case
for everyone, that while with much on our minds and hands to
accomplish but scant time and space remaining to attain the goals
we have been given or have taken upon ourselves, we measure our
breath, we race along in pursuit of the objects of our desire, those
we pursue may have long since left the track or would leave it
before we have a chance to level with them.

By the time I began to see Misa on the pretext of an evening
game twice a week, things were already on the downhill. Our queen,
whose marvellous invention it was, played the game no more, or at
least not with anyone. Misa herself had told me so, although how,
before sooner or later reaching the brink of madness one could play
with oneself a game in which duality was of the essence was

something that did not cross my mind at the time. But maybe she did not play at all, did not feel the need in the least. It is not uncommon for creators to tire of what they have brought into being. Nearly a year had passed since she had taught the game to the king, although it had been Misa to whom she had first revealed its rules and properties, months, maybe years, before the king ever heard of it. The two went along playing day upon day without anyone getting to know or being least bit taken by it, so that when the king told me about the game, and when I saw it played between Misa and him one evening, I came under its spell instantly, as if it was not an improvisation, utterly clever though it be, of the familiar rudimentary board game, but a gift I had forever coveted without once being aware of the fact. Part of the reason, which I realized only later, was that in the same instant I had also come under the spell of the girl moving the pieces, and after this momentous evening could never separate the image of one from the other in my mind.

From the room where I remain unmoving for hours, I often lose myself in the shape of the clouds that forever seem to be on the point of dissolving, untangling in stray vaporous wisps into the blue membrane of emptiness, and are yet held together by some invisible inner cohesion as they drift from one horizon to the next, measuring the vast expanse of the sky. It is the way of clouds. And not so different is our own. Meandering and dissolving through great unseen distances, wavering in a torrid, incandescent landscape where space shines like a molten mirror, where nothing is what it seems and everything is a mirage of itself, it is a mystery that we are able to take even a single step forward, transport ourselves from here to there and from there to elsewhere, without crumbling to dust or liquefying into the elements along our wayward tracks. Moving, changing, disintegrating slowly in the river rush of life.

What I could never see before, no matter how hard or close I looked, I see now in the simplest of phenomena. The most commonplace of events sometimes will lift the fug from over our thoughts, and what has accumulated by our passage through a stormy, chimeric landscape will melt away in an instant of pure lucidity, like rain in a desert, clarifying, refining the filters of vision. There begins our freedom, there, too, our terror.

The king had learnt the game on the open sea. Three full days were enough for him to learn and master the play. Perhaps the royal pair went on playing and improvising, developing further variations and openings, tiring themselves out thoroughly, so that what was chiefly meant to be a period for relaxation ended up being the arena of contest.

Their return from the sea was no different this time from those in the past. Soon enough, however, things began to alter. Within the first few months, the queen seemed to have lost all interest in the game, in time turning her back on it completely, while the king began to play with an ever burgeoning passion, first only with Misa, but then with others as well, close friends and aides among whom the new version had gained immense popularity in the shortest of time. A restlessness that hadn't been seen since his return from the far north years ago came to fill the king little by little. When playing, he would begin thoughtfully, at first making outwardly innocuous moves, absorbing any and all attacks of his opponent serenely, while managing to preserve his own reserves with the least damage to his ranks, yet by the time the game had barely developed into a middle phase, he would trap and smother the enemy's forces as and when he pleased, advancing with astonishing speed toward an endgame, and finishing him off in a fury of moves. Over the following months he had demolished any and all adversaries, Misa not excepting, although she was the most exacting of players he encountered over the board. The restiveness was not readily apparent, but to those of us who had been with him for long, it was not also entirely invisible. Was this because of a mere board game? It was silly to imagine so. Yet some hidden connection surely lay between the game and his past. Even if the game was not the cause, it was the catalyst. One thing though I had noticed, the king always played black. Could this seemingly innocent fact point to something significant? Could it be something carefully buried in his memory as a child, which as soon as it had been revealed was encouraged to be forgotten? For only that which is forgotten assails us in time with fiendish impulses.

What cannot be doubted, however, is the moment when the axis tilted completely. That was when the king's half-sister came crying to him for help, bloody and mutilated in the face. As if it was the one excuse he had been waiting for, the slight opening to thrust his foot in, he flew into a rage, stomping off as if a demon had settled on his breast. Without consulting anyone, without investigating the matter further, after all that cunning woman was not above reproach herself, forever busy hatching dirty little schemes to invite trouble, he had flown away in his vessel to carry out the accursed kidnapping.

There was hardly anything special about the meek woman the king returned with some hours hence, walking in tow, whimpering and terror-stricken, in a state of shock amid the alien splendour of the palace, perhaps even at the colour of our skin and the shape of our heads and eyes and noses. Accustomed to the slow sameness of days in the forest, the few comforts of a frugal existence in exile by the side of her spouse, she seemed as confounded among these foreign men as by the swiftness and villainy of the event itself.

None of us had moved since the king had stormed out in fury, even that wicked woman, the cause behind our future ruin, who, now that her wounds had been dressed, didn't arouse in me any sympathy. As the king entered the hall with the weeping woman trailing behind, a cruel mocking laughter rang out of her. He turned to his abductee and told her in the most matter-of-fact way to wipe off her tears and make herself at home, for this was home now, and in the same instant made her a proposal of marriage. This did not stun the woman as much as it stunned us. Although marriage by abduction was not uncommon or considered immoral in our tribe, it was something hardly expected of the king, particularly since he was only half like us, the other half of his blood answered to other customs, other rites, the social mores that bound him to the clans of the north.

Then, too, a proposal of marriage when the woman was already married, and the abduction committed not out of love or desire, but out of spite, this was against the norms, whether of north or of south, grossly improper.

What did the king see in her that none of us did? What had smitten him so? At any rate there was little in her compared to the daring allure of our own women, to say nothing of the queen. But no one questioned him, not one dared to offer his opinion, not even his brother, who subsequently resisted his every move and when things came to a head, as they were bound to do eventually, defected to the enemy camp only to return after the war and be proclaimed king, no, not even he, not at first, for in that moment each of us felt a tremor pass under our skins, something made us fear the king, who by then was a profoundly changed man, the man we had not known in years, the man we had long since forgotten.

Later, when that spy had burnt half the city to cinders, when our armies suffered one blow upon another, when one brave fighter after the next was felled by the enemy's blows and arrows, when the king in a final attempt to save the situation withdrew behind the city walls to perform the grand ritual sacrifice to propitiate the deity, the *yajña* from whose blazing fire he vowed not to separate himself until he had imbibed its fierce heat to become a being of pure flame that nothing could touch and from which the enemy would run in fear and trembling, when a handful of enemy soldiers breached the city walls to disrupt this very ritual sacrifice and distract the king, jumping from ledge to ledge, swinging from curtains and banisters, even harassing the queen, rending her robes, nearly raping her, obliging the king to break his vow, voices slowly began to murmur, as if from deep down empty wells, posing questions that seem to have no definite answers.

One blamed the kidnapping, another that devious sister of his, yet another attacked, though almost in whispers, the false pride of the king, his casual dismissal of our every misgiving, of our rising concern since the burning of the city, even the queen's repeated entreaties to set the captive free and avoid a pointless war. Indeed a priest went as far as to predict the king's end, since it was common belief that the queen's chastity was his one true shield, which, alas, had fallen at the hands of those wretched harrying savages, monkeying about with the sole aim to disrupt the sacrificial ritual, the *yajña*. As if this wasn't enough, the oracle drew a connection from some past life in which the captive was none other than the king's own daughter, and a desire to join with your daughter, in this life or another, was a sin for which even Prajāpati had not been spared.

Prajāpati had awakened from his long cosmic slumber in the dead of the night. It was always night. Only he at first, no other. From this loneliness had arisen first fear, then desire. He stared into space, and his desire made a rent in the fabric of darkness, letting in streaks of light. Thus was born his daughter, Uṣa, the dawn. The God rejoiced, for here at last was company. Instantly, without him coming to know, lost that he was in delight and desire, were born his descendants. Yet no sooner born than they wished to rid themselves of the Father's sin. Thus they sacrificed him who had engendered them. How, then, if the divination was correct, reasoned one old courtier, could the king elude a fate before which the Creator himself had yielded?

Tiresome speculation. Meaningless exchange of words carried out by fools and parasites who knew nothing better, forever playing with symbols, the one perennial pastime which was the basis of so much of our philosophy and history that we had long since forgotten their essence, content with believing the flimsiest story in the name of truth.

Because I was away in battle, and because most of the talking took place behind my back, I only heard these rumours belatedly, when there was little left to prove or salvage. Since that time though I have come to feel, whatever be the merit of these assertions, that the reason itself was far simpler. How easily we had forgotten that the king had received the boon of immortality from none other than Śiva himself, who is beyond time, and hence the one best placed to offer it. Or was it Brahmā? No, it was not a matter of honour, pride, or colour, not a matter of lust or desire, but a call of something smouldering inside, an invitation to endgame, to death. Something had taken root deep within the king's soul the moment it had been set free. For he must have known better than anyone else that what the gods grant they take away, or rather they only grant that which can be taken away. The boon after all comes with its terms, and terms are expressed in speech, and what is speech but a dark slimy tunnel through which every real intention slips past. The terms can never cover all possibilities, and so every immortality is contingent on one or another excluded event not taking place. Hence are the gods so free with boons, because in due course all things come to pass.

Did the king see then, when he heard the avalanche answering his prayers in the desert, what I see now, this image of himself falling in battle, the end of the accursed arrow sticking out from his navel, and the shining bare landscape with small triangular flags of five colours fluttering from a line stretched across it, home of homes, to which he had at last arrived?

A shadow passes over me in sleep. I look up. A crane, its legs tucked in, is catching the sun in its outstretched wings. I dream on. I am alone, the world nothing but a small empty room, a ten-by-ten-foot space, somehow glowing. In a corner, a large copper urn. Near the centre, a deity with a flowing mane, face turned away from me, stomping and swaying in a slow, surprisingly soundless dance.

XVI

TWO ANCIENT, venerable bloodlines met in the king. Two elements. Born of light and dark in equal measure, there was something of the inexplicable in him, something which resisted naming, escaping even those who knew him best.

Legend spoke of his birth on the banks of river Hir that flowed through the island of Lanka. Sumali, the king of the southern clans, dubbed by those in the north as the *Asuras* or the dark ones, wished to increase and fortify his already vast dominion, the preferred way for which was alliances formed through marriage. Toward this end, he set his sight on the sage Visravas, not only the most powerful man on earth, but the son of the great Pulastya himself, one of the ten mind-born sons of Prajāpati, now twinkling upon the world from the asterism of Big Dipper, to whom he intended to give away in marriage the hand of his daughter, Kaikesi.

While he was pondering over his plan, news came to him of the sage's visit to a hermitage in a neighbouring forest. Taking this to be a fortuitous sign, he arranged for his daughter to be noticed by Visravas just as the sage was leaving his host's cottage. Nothing more was needed on Sumali's part, he knew that if the two met, things would inevitably take the course he desired. Famed for her charm and intelligence, Kaikesi would not fail him.

Not altogether unexpectedly then, the king found Visravas walking into the royal court the very next day with a wish to seek his daughter's hand in marriage. Only too happy to oblige, the king at once announced a grand ceremony to be held in three days' time.

Filled with a sudden tenderness for this man who had received him with such humility and devotion, the sage blessed the king and promised his eternal protection to the empire and its people.

This being achieved, Sumali rested in peace and, once the wedding was over, left them undisturbed in the hut by the river, calmly watching from a distance, awaiting the birth of his grand-child.

In time the couple was blessed with a son. More children would follow. But that first child was special or was considered special. Considerate and kind, aggressive and arrogant by turn, he would grow up to be an exemplary scholar and warrior, learned in scrip-tures, reader of stars, master of the *vīṇā*. They called him Rāvaṇa, after a thought came to the mother's lips on seeing the infant, he who wins the gods by just actions, he, the lineage-bearer of sun-worshippers. Straddling two very different worlds, with one foot in the forest and the other in the palace, at home both in the pieties and rituals of his father's life and the splendour and ethics of his mother's world, he grew up into a hybrid like no other, an ascetic with the brow of a king, or a king who went around in a sage's garb, a man loved and feared equally, discoursing in two tongues, moving from observances of one realm to those of the other with uncommon ease, channelling and blending the knowledge of two distinct cultures to leap beyond into an understanding greater than either and one that was wholly unique.

Thus, later, when a struggle ensued to take control of his grand-father's empire, he was able to easily gain the support of all concerned and swiftly quell whatever slight resistance there remained in his race to the throne.

Receiving an empire that was already vast and powerful, he brought, over the years, further territories and vassal states under his control through a mix of diplomacy, mediation, and campaign. Because he was neither entirely of the north nor entirely of the south, and of each side in part, many clans identified with him, either out of fear or out of awe, and he was able to bridge the chasm that had forever divided the two races, earning the respect of even those who ruled on the far edges of the world.

But what on the outside joined him to both sides, divided him internally. The deep axe-wound of exile, of homelessness, a fate no hybrid can escape, for it is not of the world but of the mind, unless you take the two to be one and the same, inseparable. As the world contracted before his eyes to something solid and manageable, a tear opened somewhere inside past which a steady stream of diffusion seeped and spread. With the woman he loved beside him and with no kingdom left within sight to conquer, his gaze turned back to probe its very source. First uncertainty, then boredom, then restlessness grew in him. And so came the day when without a word to anyone except his queen and two or three trusted ministers and even to them offering only a tentative sketch of his desire, he slipped out of the palace late one night.

The queen did not once demur when she heard his wish. Only a few years of marriage and she too longs for the gap that is about to open, less a distancing than an acknowledgment of the void into which the ferocity of their feelings had quietly vanished, the void which is the slow, cruel turning of days and years, the millstone whose heavy measured rotation grinds every ambition, every meaning to dust.

At each step away from the city, the ruler in him dies a little and the wanderer awakes, groaning and blinking, or better still, it is the wandering spirit of his childhood that has lain sleeping in the shade for who knows how long.

He heads north, following an instinct, the paths of the past, in the memory of his father, whom he has not seen in years and of whose whereabouts he has not the slightest idea, but also because he cannot go further south before soon encountering the ocean, overfamiliar, billowing with pointless activity, past which there is nothing but more swells, and then ice, teeming with beings that accept his sovereignty, live in his protection.

It is north he must go, retrace his steps across a continent he has patiently sculpted with all his ambition, tact, and fury, although now like a commoner, like a mendicant traveller if it comes to that, covered in dust with calloused palms and ankles, free of his banners and regalia, his elephants and armies, so that no one gives him a moment's attention even as he notices everyone and everything.

By the time night falls again, he has been walking without a single halt for a whole day in the forest, his strength on the ebb and mind grown vacant. He finds himself next to a mud hut of a recluse or an ascetic, its low walls a pale blue in the filigree light of the moon flashing through leaves and branches. He asks for water and a place to rest, settling down on the ground against the wall. He drinks from a gourd and his upturned jaw through which the water trickles is blue in the blue of the air. The ascetic hands him a pipe filled with hemp and he is grateful for it. Never having been one for words, he leisurely drags in silence the lush vapours into his lungs to the point of bursting. He thinks nothing, or rather no thought comes to him, not even the memory of his own steps on the forest floor, not even the dry scratching of thorns and shrubs all over his legs and ankles, not the birdsong he has heard throughout the day, not the wind in the trees.

When he is shown into the hut, he shuffles about briefly in the gloom, trying to ascertain his bearings. A floor of beaten mud cracking in places, a much scoured copper pot, two or three spoons, a wooden ladle, half-rotten and losing shape, a pail, a gourd, walls lined with soot. Low flames hissing in a clay stove built in a corner leave a gloss on the dark which is otherwise complete. The anchorite hands the traveller something to eat, the taste of ash and salt, and turns away to douse the fire for the night.

He stretches himself out where he has been sitting and soon sleep lies heavy on him, while his host sits on his haunches in the dark, silent, motionless, his eyes, yellowed from melancholy, hardship or illness, fixed and sparkling like embers deep in a grate.

He is up at dawn, but his host is already in the open, working a small vegetable patch at the rear of the hut. He watches him awhile as the other pulls out a few potatoes and green shoots from the ground unaware that he is being observed. When he finally approaches the traveller, he has in his arms a melon, which he breaks open on a stone and of which he offers one half to his guest. If the older one suspects something in his bearing or manner he doesn't say so, and for the first time there occurs a brief exchange, more a careful barter of words, revealing hardly anything significant, yet to ears trained to register subtle inflexions, eyes that catch the hint, nothing more perhaps is necessary.

Soon he is on his way. The spontaneous and natural generosity he has received this past night he should not expect so readily to find in future. But the kindness is also the kindness of nature and of those who are close to it and he moves in its protection, every day walks deeper into its fold. He emerges from the trees and treads in open grasslands, waist deep through shafts that bend in the wind, shine golden like waves on the sea. He startles a hare and swiftly snatches it away from the wild grass, wringing its neck and hanging it from his shoulder. To the west the terrain rises into the rocks, and it is to them that he heads in search of a cave to rest for the night. Now he is walking straight into a swollen and distended sun that trembles and drips into space like molten wax, the colour of blood. Near where the climb snakes into the crags, he halts at a pond where egrets watch him from serrated boulders. Along the gravel path winding upward, he collects sticks to build a fire.

Night finds him sitting on a rock at the mouth of a crevice into which he will crawl and be safe from the wind that is growing ever fierce by the minute. To one side he has built a low fire upon which the soft flesh of the hare he recently flayed lies roasting and crackling. The cold makes his eyes water and the dark passes through this teary sieve to explode at the far edge in a shower of light. They fall, the stars, in wide arcs along the curve of outer space and are instantly born anew back above in the heavens. Later, when he slips into the stony gap like a snake, he hears the wind breaking against the rocks, receding, breaking again, as if the earth itself is drawing and expelling breath. For a while he follows its rhythm, lying flat on his back, slowing the beat of his heart to the heartbeat of the world. He feels neither fatigue nor the need for sleep, in fact his mind is calm and alert, utterly empty. Now and then as the wind changes its course, in the brief perfect silence that reigns in the air, he hears faintly the wolf-howls from the edge of the jungle, a half-day's march behind him.

At noon the next day he enters the water, wades through it knee-deep, acutely aware of the currents or the slightest of declines under foot, difficult to detect by the eye, that in no time could transfer him to the centre of a treacherous whirlpool. He knows his way well through water, through the bare, uninhabited islets that are to follow one another between slim, fluid intervals, for he has crossed and re-crossed this route countless times in the past, on his trips and campaigns to the north, but always at a remove, always on horseback, on boats or elephants, and never on foot, never like this skirting danger so close, gasping for breath at every other step, never immersed waist deep in the sea, the colour and abundance of its life seething about him.

On and on it goes, land giving way to water and water turning back on the land's edge, for a day and a night and beyond, while he lives on frugal supplies of food and drink. Thirsty and hungry he finally steps upon the peninsula and for a moment it seems that the entire continent is tilting under the weight of his parched soles. Or is it he who bends forward, his centre of gravity sinking down the perineum?

He moves on, and the land or his feet slowly find a new equilibrium. Too fast has he gone in the past, with too much on his mind, and it is so that he is seeing this landscape for the first time. Soon enough he walks into a grove, picks up and bites hungrily into the fruit that lies strewn everywhere. He comes upon a settlement and the tribesfolk, taking him to be a holy mendicant, seek his blessings, bringing him first pudding and buttermilk, and then a dish of rice-balls in a thin sulphur-yellow curry, strong and savoury, with a hint of coconut. They offer him lodgings and he decides to stay for the night.

He is woken up by the scuffle of feet, sounds of something resembling a skirmish, a woman's wail, the restless beat of a horse's hooves. He is out of the hut in no time. Outside it is a scene of mayhem. A thatch is burning, shooting balls of fire into the sky. Bandits. One comes charging straight at him, pike in hand. He leaves him in the mud, the blade deep in the victim's breast, blood spreading under his convulsing form that is fast growing cold. He pulls another down from his horse and finishes him with two solid blows of his hand, breaking the rogue's neck with the second. He takes the sword of the one fallen and climbs onto the horse. He kills three, maybe four of the attackers, and the remaining flee in terror from his demonic wrath.

He dismounts at last and the tribesmen are around him, kneeling down in a circle, children and women closing in from behind, seeking his protection. Is he not already their protector, the final protector past a series of protectors? Did he not promise safety to these lands and their people when he brought them under his dominion long ago? No, he is too far, too high up to make good the pledge of his protection to those who need it, those at the far reaches of his empire, those who so openly share their food and dwelling with him, their king. It is only now, perhaps for the first time, that he has acted as a true sovereign. But it is too late, too different now. He is in search of something else. For the moment he can do no more. And he cannot halt his journey here, though where he is headed he knows not.

He leaves before dawn, moving northward but at a slant to the east. And even at that slant, his path makes other slants, so that when he travels through the forest he ends up on the crags by the beach and when he walks along the shore, the sand shining like steel and the water a dull grey, rippling past his gaze, he reverts to the lush comfort of trees again. He steers clear of people and soon he vanishes like a column of smoke into the landscape. For days, for months, he turns invisible.

When one sees him next, he is much changed. The elements have had time to work upon him. His skin has gone coppery, even leathery in places, indeed stretches taut over his bones such that he looks gaunt from certain angles and his eyes, deep set in their sockets, have a reddish gleam in them. His hair, long and matted, coils into a topknot over the dome of his skull, and his beard is brown and dense. He is living near the mangrove forest which sprawls over an immense alluvial delta through which the Ganga passes on its slow, meandering course to the bay. There, near a pond, is a cluster of huts, where the adepts live, a community of men and women who spend their days practicing arcane rituals, asceticism and alchemy. It is the cult of the goddess, the dark one. With them he has settled and is seen at dawn sitting before the square brick altar, performing oblations and intoning hymns to the god of fire. Each day he goes farther into this world of arcana, a world of flesh and dream, of breath, fire, and mercury, ringed in by the sea-forests, by majestic crocodiles, elephants, and tigers, by friendly dolphins and birds of the air, by bands of rhinos and wild buffalo, by greedy scavengers.

For some time now, a dog has kept him company, follows him everywhere, at times running back and forth, at other times moving in circles around his moving form, like a planet tied to a shifting sun. At night, it sleeps with him, huddled together on a deer's pelt inside the outmost hut. On moonless evenings, when ceremonies for the goddess take place, when the drum booms and the flames cut fiery swoops on the air, when metal enters bodies and flesh meshes with flesh, pure terror shines in the animal's eyes, and it is afraid of the master it so loves, in fear it mewls like a kitten, before going completely still. In those nights, as he dreams of a tiger decimating herds of bison in open grasslands, and later riding the same tiger over snow-blocked passes, the dog sits on its hind limbs, cowed and shivering in a corner.

At the onset of spring, he again treads north, and the animal is glad for it. Through fields of maize and barley, golden under the noon sky, he observes the diffused outline of the first hills. At first hardly a smudge on the horizon, their form grows clearer with each step, acquires weight, until he can see beyond a mustard field, yellow on green, the sheer slate-blue bulk of the mountains, snow etched in their folds, rising from the earth's womb. He, his dog following, heads straight toward them and reaching the top of a knoll he watches from a breach in the pines the rays of the declining sun throwing them into stark relief.

He moves through wave upon wave of oaks, pines, and walnut trees, through a forest of rhododendrons oozing red blossoms, through mighty cedars and evergreens that block the sun and make the air cold and damp, past lakes that shine like molten silver in the clear light of the moon, and it is so that he is no closer to those tall peaks cutting into the sky in all their silence and splendour. He looks for food and the dog looks with him, sometimes splitting away on its own, but returning always to share its find with him.

On the sixth day, he has left the tree line behind and the landscape grows rocky and bare before him, there is snow by the wayside, with only eagles for company, and they too few and distant, soaring and circling in the thin air over the summits, and suddenly he is upon the high mountains, skirting along a foot-wide track at the edge of a vertiginous gorge that collects the terrible echo of the river gushing hundreds of feet below. At dusk, he hits upon a nomad trail and soon finds a group making camp on a high plateau by the edge of a small lake. He joins up with them and although he understands nothing of their dialect, he is given a bowl of soup with mutton fat in it, his dog likewise, and is ushered toward the campfire. Under a heavy canopy of stars, with the fire crackling in the logs and the tribe's wild shaggy oxen tinkling their bells and releasing puffs of breath from their shiny muzzles, very white against the chill of the night air, he sits with the rest of the group that is singing or talking in whispers. The dog curls up in the hollow of his legs, and he stares long into its wet eyes, the fatigue visible in them, perhaps even the first signs of illness, and deep in their solitary island, he hums softly to it.

Early at dawn the nomads break camp, and he goes with them, falls in line behind one of the couples, their young daughter, a child really, observing him from the back of an ox, never letting him out of her sight. Men and beasts go slowly in file up the mountain. A night passes, half a day. Now there is ice everywhere, although it is beginning to thaw in places. The track lies frozen, and they inch ever cautiously up the pass full of snow. Within an hour's march from the night camp, his dog had coughed up blood, and because it kept faltering and falling behind more and more as the ascent steepened, he now walks with the animal resting across his shoulders and he feels its laboured breath on the nape of his neck.

Wherever the sight travels, there are just mountains. Fold upon fold of rock and ice, a feeble sun skipping through tatters of cloud. He walks in a kind of daze, in a spell cast by some mountain spirit, and he is long past the top of the pass, can already make out a beige landscape merging with the bluest sky in the distance, when the form girdling his neck suddenly feels cold and heavy. No throb, no pulse reaches him from the animal's flesh, and he hopes that it left him at the high point of the path, up there in the clouds.

He keeps descending as before, holding the dead animal up close. If the others notice, they say nothing. The girl has gone to sleep on the back of the ox, its blanketed hump her pillow. At a bend in the road stands a cairn with an old flag fluttering from its crest, and it is here that he leaves the carcass for the birds that depend on it.

They go down fast now, on the other side of the mountain face, and the dry earth stretches before them into a lunar wilderness. Crags raising their shoulders above the low shrubs that cover them, meadows and patches of grass watered by thin icy channels where agile, skittish goats graze in their own blue radiance, and soon there are not even shrubs, only cactus-like plants and rocks that glisten with quartz and salt. Dry, loose earth wraps the unending landscape in a mantle of ochre and brown, and tiny round stones scrunch underfoot. The tall peaks of the Himalaya refract like crystals behind them.

When they are on the high plains again, the caravan halts. The sun declines in the west and they decide to pitch camp for the night. This is the final stop before the group splits. The larger of the two will continue north the next day, while those remaining will turn west. It is west he will go. By a happy coincidence the family he has become familiar with over the past few days heads west too. He has picked up enough of their strange speech to make meaning from the short low grunts and gestures that do service for words here.

Night falls like a clap from heaven and a fierce chill reigns, stars glitter sharp and cold like jewels and the sky is of a black that shines with its own darkness. By the fire he sits, sipping the dry, heady liquor that leaves in its wake a taste of burnt wood in the mouth. By now used to his presence among her kind, the child crawls into his lap and he slowly sings her to sleep.

A few days pass like this, the camp growing ever smaller, and members branching out like streams from a river, until at last he is on his own again, walking forever west, toward the place where, it is said, creation first sprang forth. Toward Lake Manasa, its waters the cosmic flux of the universe, the fluid mind of Brahmā, to the source of all life he travels, which, because he too comes from it, is his own source, his own antecedence. Isn't he the grandson of Pulastya, born of Brahmā's mind just like the lake?

And yet it is not to his source alone he goes, but to his end too. For past Manasarovar, remote in its astral sphere, above a wave of brown hills, floats Kailas, the visible earthly speck of the invisible Meru, the pivot of the universe, which no mortal can glimpse and live to tell the tale, at least not in words intelligible to anyone. On Kailas, older than the oldest mountains, dwells Rudra, god of death and destruction, and all that lies beyond them. Śiva, the supreme yogi, god beyond gods, lives on its highest slope, turned into himself in eternal silence. He alone is worthy of prayer, he who is untouched by time, the timeless one, destroying and reviving the world in the blink of an eye.

He walks in a country of planetary uniqueness. Here the sun burns in all its might, yet the cold is relentless. The wind funnels through far away rocks and crashes against glacial parapets with all its force but it is so that there is no sound and the silence is ever deeper, seems to have no bottom. Sometimes the trill of a lark reaches him, or the long melancholy groan of a crane, and this too is a form of silence. Here the leopard hunts on padded feet, and the ibex leaves no trace. Distances stretch and contract, refract and multiply endlessly and time is meaningless. He goes along the river, its bed silted with gold, and it seems to wither away into the bare, sandy landscape, but the further he walks, the further its source appears to be. What seems close is far, and what looks far is suddenly there. Across the river, hillocks appear now and then, mounds really, pockmarked with caves and gravel pits. To his left forever, the chain of the Himalaya, their eternal snows a prism of light. He knows of their origin. How the god once awoke from his cosmic slumber at the summit of Kailas and roared with laughter. A shudder went through the earth and the crust cracked and split in a million places, drifted away from sheer force and then recoiled, colliding and rising in folds to stupendous heights, lending vapour the touch of stone, eclipsing Kailas itself. The might of pure, uninhibited laughter.

He wades through the river, gold dust sticking to his ankles, in search of a place to rest for the night, juniper shrubs bursting through shale, lining the crevices along the climb. He enters a cave, its mouth a sliver between jagged piles of stone. Inside, the smell of dust and mould, a whiff of charred wood trapped in the cave's perfect eternity, its sloping rock roof, black behind the black of old soot. Half wedged in stone, hanging limp, a piece of red sash. Absence. He finds it suitable for his purpose, plans to settle here for a certain duration, to think, meditate, perform rituals, to deepen his knowledge of the arcana.

Enveloped in darkness he sits for many dawns and many dusks, and when next he blinks a thin stream of light floods his pupils and he cannot say if he still holds onto his flesh or melted away long ago, whether in fact he awakes in the world from which he turned and not another. Then vague shimmering forms begin to emerge in this gash of light, and he slowly distinguishes the air from the river and river from the peak above, all as if of molten silver yet grading in contrast from one to the other. He stands up, walks out of the cave, cuts through the river and flies straight to the nearest peak. But his body refuses to budge, for his legs have remained crossed for so long that no blood flows into them and the cells seem to have asphyxiated. He moves his palms in circles over his knees, uses the strength that remains in his arms to separate and stretch them open on the ground. He imagines the blood flowing from his head downward, right to the tip of his toes, then pulls himself up against the rock. He feels no pain. After he has stood thus awhile, he is able to move his foot and toes at the joints. He takes slow steps toward the source of light. Soon he is coming down the dirt track, over rocks and shale, the river in his eyes. The cold doesn't touch him and the sun shines through a soft halo. He remembers his past life in its entirety, but it has now receded to a mere speck stuck to the arc of his skull that rings in a space of utter emptiness.

His frame has become lean from lack of food, but he walks with an assured stride, his eyes deep and blazing, such that as he wades through the water, the leopard by the bank abandons its kill and fades into the wilderness. Further still, the earth seems to contract in a painter's palette. He lifts the still warm gazelle onto his shoulder and walks in search of nettles. He likes this place. The mounds, the cave, the river sprawling across the green and russet landscape and, at the far end, the mountains, silent, eternal, cloaked in their own ice-mists.

For days, for months, he does nothing but stare at the view before him, until all that is without is also within. His rations are plain and meagre. Sallowthorn, nettles, a lump of salt, cool water to drink. On some nights, he collects juniper twigs to build a fire and, when the mood is upon him, chants the hymns of the Sāma Veda with a deep emotion. Master of the lute, master now of the subtle winds travelling through his body, he pulls taut an arm such that the veins rise up from his spare flesh, and he presses and plucks them as if they were so many strings over the frets.

In time he is on the move again. Now come the days of rapture, days of delirium. Days of trudging where nothing moved but he. The river angles away to his right, and the bulwark of high peaks seems to slant leftward. They too, it appears, are abandoning him, and he walks into the desert opening wide at his feet. Above him, in the blue of the firmament, a skein of geese, as if replicating the features of the landscape, flies west too. He drinks frugally from his make-do flask, and chews a few green twigs for nourishment. His mind seems to be anchored to the flesh by the flimsiest of bonds, yet he pays no attention to either, he, who watches the watcher, that which watches the I.

For three days he walks without cease, and in the early evening of the fourth he glimpses from the corner of his eye a band of blue as if alight. He walks toward it enchanted. After almost an eternity he sees the first signs of life, of wild asses grazing along its near shore, bold and prepossessing in their serenity. The mind-lake comes into view in an arc of indigo tempered with ice-floes that continually shudder and splinter and cave in from their own weight, creating a terrible symphony of sounds. He is observing the elements in their purest form, in ceaseless activity and collision. The tumult of the celestial crush which not ten, not a hundred battle-fields could match. The lake roars and groans, he can hear cries of human agony and the melancholy moans of a thousand conches and the deep boom of the war drums rising from it. In the depthless silence of the desert, the lake acts as a counterpoint.

He slowly climbs up a promontory of sparkling rocks only to find that these are whole plateaux of congested snow as old and firm as the land itself. He walks on and is presently skirting mudflats where gulls and sand martins roam with ever-alert eyes. He falls into a pit and instantly the warmth of the earth pervades his every pore and in its bosom he falls to sleep.

In the legend revealed to him in childhood, the lake is his kin, a distant brother or sister, and in spite of the ice which the waves thrust inshore, its water feels warm against the skin. He lifts his hand away and a spoonful of it settles in the hollow of his palm, the surplus dribbling through his curled fingers. He mumbles a few words invoking Brahmā and quickly sucks in the lake's nectar from the base of the palm, feeling it slowly trickle down and settle near his navel, insubstantial like vapour and yet ever present like a cosmic fragment from the god's mind.

Cured of hunger, thirst, and fatigue, he suddenly feels himself immortal, the benisons of heaven circulating in his system. When he walks out of the lake, his tread is lighter than air, and he seems to cover substantial ground at each step without noticing. There is in him a sense of accomplishment, though what he has accomplished he cannot say. Yet he feels he has found his one true home, and wherever he goes it will go with him.

Now the bank rises steeply away from the lake and he chances upon a cave scooped from stone and pink-coloured debris. The lake lies beneath him, foaming under a chiaroscuro of snow-white clouds and deep brown mountains. Is it a swan he sees?, a goose?, calmly sailing over its indigo sheen. Or is it only a rock of ice? Perhaps it is Śiva himself, come down from Kailas to take his leisure in the divine waters.

There are hot springs nearby and sometimes he slips into them, lying still for hours, eyes locked onto the faintly visible snow cone of Kailas, rising above its own mandala of dark sandy hills, its black granite shining in the form of a step-ladder where the slant is sheer and the snow cannot take hold. Adepts believe it is a stairway to other worlds, and one from which the mountain-god himself comes down. Here, too, sometimes he boils fish that he finds shored against the lake's edge, their lives descended into the water's immensity. A single boiled morsel can keep hunger at bay for days. Daily he follows the moon's cycle and reads the stars, making complex calculations in his head.

He is slowly drifting westward again, en route to the mountain itself. Late one afternoon he has his first sighting of the other lake, opening in a sweeping crescent away from him, its water the colour of a peacock's tail, a cloud bank forever hanging above, throwing most of it into perpetual shade and the relief of the land rising and breaking in support of its eerie beauty. This is the dark god's altar. Blessed or not, here he must perform severe penance for his gruesome acts, for the blood he has shed in the past, before the mountain will welcome him.

For nine full nights, he sits by its shore, his flesh feverish from the mind's heat. On the tenth, when a sickle-shaped moon settles upon the mountain's left flank, he slits a finger and lets the blood fall into the ink-black water of the lake. The drops fall slowly against the shining sliver of the moon, dissolving in a sharp hiss at the point of contact, as if they did not share the same fluid form but were hard glowing coals extinguishing in brief violent gasps. Just when the last drop falls into the lake, the ritual concluded, a snowstorm breaks over the mountain's southern face, signalling the success of the sacrifice. He knows this for the granite steps rising sharp from the seeming softness of snow shine clearer than before as if embossed over its white immensity for his sake alone.

He is stirred by this phenomenon. Overcome by the darkness that lies dormant in him and which the lake reflects like his own subconscious, he raises its water to his cold, cracked lips on a sudden impulse. A tremor, a sting, goes through them, for the water is utterly saline, even bitter. Bile rises in his throat and he steers away, retching.

Between the two lakes, the first the source of life and the second forever lifeless, is the path that heads to Kailas, and it is there he goes. The night seems endless, and he is soon scaling the mountain slope, rising sheer into the sky's depth. Slow and stumbling he inches upward, fighting for purchase on the slippery rocks, each step of the stone ladder hundreds of feet apart, until just before dawn, halfway from the summit, the crescent moon hangs an arm's length away, Śiva's powerful sickle out there for the taking. A slow howl breaks from his throat, which is tinged blue, perhaps because of the opaline beams that break on the snow, perhaps because he is possessed by the fearsome god himself who is this very moment pouring *his* essence in the concavity of his soul. The howl now is a terrifying roar. And this too is a meaning of his name, Ravana. He, of the thunderous roar.

He does not hear or see the avalanche building behind him, and it finds him unaware, carrying him down to the foot of the mountain and beyond in a raging torrent of ice.

He awakes far off in the wilderness. How he got here he does not know. He picks himself up and begins to walk. He follows no set direction, roving in the desert like a madman.

After months he comes upon a place strangely familiar from some half-forgotten memory. This could have been a settlement, although not permanent. Now nothing remains, only signs of ruin and abandonment, if ruin, that is, can come to that which is itself transient. For a while he moves about the place. A few discarded objects, a charred pole, here and there pegs driven into the ground still clutching half-burnt ropes, scattered, dust-ridden utensils, a necklace of cowrie shells, the half-eaten corpse of a woman. Not a touch of emotion he feels, walks impassively across the site as if the whole world was a charnel ground.

He reaches a hillock and crouches beneath the overhang of a rock. He sits very still. All at once, he is aware of movement. But when he scans the surroundings there is nothing. Then a shuffle of steps. The tread of a child, light, nervous, even fearful. He explores no further, banishes the thought from his mind.

In the evening, he builds a small fire, shielding it with round stones, baking the last ration of tubers he carries on him. The flames throw jagged, dancing shadows on the near wall. He watches them

XVI

awhile. Then he sees one shadow separate from the tangled mass and grow still. He turns to look the other way. The child is beside him, smeared in dirt, slight abrasions on her arms and chin, clothes in tatters, observing his profile without curiosity, as if she knows something about him that he will never know himself.

XVII

HIDDEN AND scattered amidst the plenitude of life, dreams and objects lie in wait for us. It is to them, or rather to a few among them, that we are forever inching unaware, sketching our personal cartographies onto the world as we go along, rounding the bends like a rope curling on the pegs, marking our one true territory on land and water, on matter and mind. But in the never relenting movement of time and fate, it is only natural that these first encounters leave no trace of recognition in us, no impression of their significance or the soon-to-be-exerted totemic power in our locked and struggling lives.

So it was with the king when he first saw the queen's game. They had been drifting out of the bay all evening under the slow push of a south-west wind, and the royal craft now near stationary was rocking gently on the waves. The moon recently risen appeared to head straight for the constellation of Cetus, but down here in the ocean its light was washing over the wet backs of whales that had come up to draw breath and emit short vaporous jets into the air. He had been watching from beneath the billowing sails these magnificent beings born under the constellation's sign, and like him shaped and nurtured by two elements. He has always felt a certain closeness with them, a kinship difficult to define, for what could connect him to these fortresses of flesh trailing their vast bulks in the open horizons of the sea? And yet it is for their sake alone that he makes this voyage each year, succumbs again and again to the water's lure.

Still under the dark, diaphanous clutch of the night, it was inevitable that he would fail to register the full weight of the moment in which he first saw the checked board and the two miniature immobile armies, surprisingly slim and shorn of all but the more symbolic of distinguishing features. Nor did he later think much of this initial encounter, for by then the game and its working had so subtly and completely pervaded his judgment that defeat and death in life was just another endgame in the binary universe of the board.

Ever since the queen had finished improving and perfecting the technical aspects of play, her attention had turned to its outward form. Once every few weeks, a fresh set of pieces was delivered to her, appropriately modified as per her wishes, but she had scarcely begun to take joy in their craftsmanship, when errors would jump out of their design and conception, spoiling her momentary delight. Still bulky, needlessly ornate, overwrought, she would repeat time and again to the chief artisan, sketching for his benefit upon the air what was even to her but faintly discernible. What she had been unable to propose at once was the idea of replacing the image with its symbol. Only this she knew, that to maintain the balance of its enhanced possibilities the pieces had to reflect the swiftness and ease of the game's new lines and movements, and the imagistic figures of old were of little help here. As a consequence, the visible side of the game changed gradually into something that at first glance was near unrecognizable from its ancient prototype. Not surprising if one thinks how with each new ruler on the throne, the kingdom and its emblems, its architecture and artefacts, indeed the most common of objects like keys and bells and pottery, underwent such slow and subtle transformations that in a matter of years what the kingdom projected to a returning traveller was something perceptibly different from the picture lodged in memory.

Nearly half a hand in length, tapering out from an identical round base into disparate shapes at their crests, the pieces stood in their beige or ochre squares at the opposite ends of the board, here a pale white in colour and there a shining ebony, horses, elephants, and ships flanking the slightly taller, crowned but otherwise featureless, heads of king and queen at the centre, with a low line of footmen in front, alert and watchful like sentinels. Two full armies ready for battle.

And yet when the board caught his eye, the profile of the queen motionless above it, the king simply imagined this to be a model of imminent engagement between two sides, at best a symbolic and beautifully crafted showpiece, attractive though lifeless, soon to take its place on the shelf among many of its kind, and growing ever inert each day under the gaze of habit. Think then of his surprise when he realized that the pieces were not fixed but moveable. Instinctively, he grabbed the white horse and advanced it like in the old game, jumping over the pawn in front to lay it in the third square to the right from its original position. And with this oblique leap of the horse dawned on him the enormous thrust the game had been given by dint of the queen's ingenuity alone, and his eyes shone with fresh interest, even admiration. A single reflex, and his intuition had revealed half of the departures to him, already the dice was useless, forgotten, the will supreme, in control and at work everywhere.

Now she saw once more the man who had been languishing for so long under the growing burden of his thorny, elevated position. She had watched how bit by bit, almost against his own wish, life of the palace, concerns of the throne, had reclaimed him from the solitary state in which he had returned from his travels years ago. That nobility of being which was not his by birth or breeding alone, but was acquired through fierce hardships and learning had been slowly pervaded and in the end snuffed out by the desires and worries of those around him. Men, it was said, become intoxicated by that in which they live, come to resemble their environment gradually and completely. But for the present his interest had been kindled, and for her this was enough.

The queen spoke freely, as if picking up a conversation from before. They sat facing one another across the round table, behind their respective armies, white for him, black for her. The square of the board inside the ring of the table, containing every conceivable geometric design, visible or as yet hidden, like an arcane, enchanting mandala. She explained the rules, connecting the newly modelled pieces to their counterparts in the old game, their wider sweep over the board, their new positions and heightened ability to thrust and parry, attack and retreat.

Engrossed in the board's force field from the start, sucked into its symmetry, at once elementary and perfect, the king simply nodded each time as she gently pressed the tip of her forefinger on the top of a piece in the back row pronouncing its name. Elephant. Horse. Ship. King. Queen. Ship. Horse. Elephant. Inwardly noting their names and positions, perhaps already planning the first moves, he did not even look up at the mention of the word *queen*, the only piece lacking antecedence. He had taken her place and powers on the board for granted, and for the first time she felt herself coming abreast of him on the battlefield, staring at the danger openly at his side, restless to show her mettle, his equal at last a shade ahead even, felt in that instant all real or imagined past wrongs righted, the perennial wait and frustration of being left behind now ended forever.

They began instantly, the first of the many games to be played in the course of two nights and a day on the royal board. She was astonished at the speed with which he moved, how quickly he picked up the faults, squared the wrong advances, his attention unwavering over the pieces, the joy of lifting their small frames between his fingers, their slight heaviness strangely comforting, adding to the pleasure. For once he was not issuing orders from afar, abstracted from reality, but participating in it, forming it, resisting it, leaving his mark. Not vested in the figure of the king alone, his spirit animated every piece, split sixteen ways, filled horse, pawn, and queen alike, letting them loose over the board. Fault lines emerged and faded away continually, and danger lay concealed in the greatly contrasting movement of pieces, for if some were harmless at a distance, the power of others did not diminish in the least due to their remoteness from the site of action, indeed they smote just when one was not covering one's back. A few met and clashed and were swept off. Footmen hobnobbed with elephants and cavalry, traversing dark and light ground with relative ease, while ships sailed off locked in their fawn or ochre diagonals, one drifting cautiously in the dark and the other racing boldly across bands of light.

The players projecting their passions, hopes, and fears onto the board between them. Yet even as they spread their nets, meshing and enmeshing each other in their skill and cunning, who is it that acts through them, weighing and demolishing attacks and positions, devising fresh permutations with fiendish virtuosity, choosing from an infinite number of invisible moves occurring around each move, every moment? For what unfolds here takes its cue from numerous other moves that are being played out elsewhere, intuiting effects and consequences that cannot for now be measured or seen.

The queen's hand, the big emerald sparkling from it, makes the clinching move. Although the king has lost, he shows next to no emotion, not a sign of unease or vexation given his intense involvement a moment ago. If anything, there is in him, if one cares to look closely, a stroke of delight, coupled with a justifiable pride in his so swiftly acquired understanding of play, his first tentative rendition. And what is more, he is already looking ahead.

Barely had the board been emptied, barely had the queen sunk deeper into the armchair, than he began to arrange the pieces afresh. Rematch? She was half-expecting this. What was it about the game that did not let one be? This was never the case earlier, where the players' interest would begin to flag toward the end, the throws of the dice becoming quicker, more impatient. But now win or loss, the player was forced, almost against the will, to ask for a rematch. To lose here was to disgrace yourself utterly, as much as in battle, if not more, for here it was solely your own doing, your own responsibility. Like gambling, with which it had absolutely nothing else in common, victory was always round the bend, just outside the grasp. And the need for victory was unrelenting, the self, fortified in its own fiction, hungering for it. Fate or no fate, the chase was of the same nature. So they played again, and he lost again. Then a third time.

By mid-morning they were playing once more, in the shade fanned out from the sails, the wet breeze on their faces and the sea about them a bed of molten silver. In each of the games of the past night, the king had opened with a different piece, and now he was going still further. How much of an impression the game had made on him, she could see easily, how quickly the new format had replaced the old, the pattern emerging in the very first moves alone making the earlier version look like a child's ludo. Near evening, however, she was starting to suspect something else. Not excitement or interest or the flourishing desire for victory, but another, darker feeling, deeper too, residing too close to the sinew.

The king had recently won his first game, and the pieces were back on the board. They had returned to the cabin, to their armchairs, talking. Outside it was night. But the king was only half-listening, stealing glances at the unopened game before him, restless for engagement one more time. Useless to talk, thought the queen, as long as these tiny men hold him in their close grip. But it was not the pieces themselves that bewitched the king. It was the feeling of control and supremacy spreading out of the board, overflowing into the world, a feeling he had first accepted wholeheartedly and naturally, then resisted and annulled, only to later succumb to it, little by little, almost without his knowledge, in the slow, cruel roll of nights and days through the royal corridors, under the ever growing burden of sovereign pleasures and duties. And now life had come full circle, the fiction of the self complete and perfect. Nothing to do, thought she, but to go on with it, and spoke the simple and obvious but, given the line of thinking the king was silently pursuing, also portentous words. Shall we play?

She had returned to black, and he opened with the queen's pawn. She responded likewise, and soon the two pawns stood blocking each other in the middle of the board. He then advanced the ship's pawn on the queen's flank, to which she replied with her king's pawn. Then the white horse on the queen's side jumped forward, backing the ship's pawn advanced previously. In quick response, the black king's horse came forth, covering the back of the first moved pawn in the middle of the board. Opening in the middle, but building support from the side, the forces spread along the diagonal axis of the board like a stream, here white with snow and there deep, dark, primordial. He thought a moment, then dropped his other horse, the one on the king's side, into the game, bring it in line with the first horse, stationed a mere two squares away. The queen replied by sliding the ship to the square in front of the king. Now he planned the first attack, sending his queen's ship across enemy lines to challenge the dark horseman as if to a duel, both parties ready with their respective seconds, the white ship backed by a horse and the ebony horse in turn seconded by a ship, as if each party was confronting its image in a mirror, strangely distanced and trans-formed in colour. The stream was beginning to tumble and swell over the board. In quick succession, infantry, horses, and elephants stirred into action. Every piece backed by another, the check-field for a moment looked staid, if entangled. Now it was impossible to move further without first striking, and thus on his next move, the king took a pawn with a pawn, an attack which was duly answered by the queen with one of her own pawns. New lines were estab-lished, and some of the space freed for fresh combat. The king pounced upon the opportunity, pushing his queen into the fray, advancing the piece like a ship along its light diagonal to the leftmost edge of the board, reining it in just before the enemy lines. In response the queen's ship inched one step forward in the direction of the enemy queen. Emboldened by the thrust of the game, the king pushed his as yet unused ship flanking his own king right up to the adversary's ranks, blocking off the dark ship's route to one side. But the queen was not to be deterred at her own gates, and she swept away the enemy ship with her own. Hardly had the surviving ship rested in its new square than the white queen came rushing and took it off the board. She changed course and the unmoved pawn of the recently removed ship sprang into action at the far end. By now the king seemed unstoppable, mounting attack on attack, slaying her horse with his second ship on the other side of the game only to lose it in turn to her other horse, then shifting his attention to the centre once more, using one of his pawns to take an enemy pawn, and then in turn being swept away by its second. Although both sides had been continuously on the offensive, their armies appeared suddenly in retreat, with a wide gap opening in the middle from left to right, and two isolated black pawns hanging in its immensity. But soon there were reinforcements. More men were shoved into the kiln of battle, and when one's gaze wavered past the other's ranks, one found the rival king safely withdrawn behind his pawns, as if mirroring one's own steps in the plaid world of the game. She presently found her horseman straight in the enemy queen's line of attack, the piece being doubly dangerous, for it was but a step away from infiltrating her own ranks. So she sent the black queen to block its advance and force a retreat. Then the respective elephants moved sideways, confronting each other from the opposite ends of the board, discouraged from attacking by a lone pawn in the middle of their path. On and on it went, the steadily advancing pawns, the hopscotching horsemen, the quick-footed queen. Then another impasse, then a sudden slaughter, then a play of elephants, moving in teams, then an elephant against a horse, then a few casualties, then silence, silence before the storm, then the storm, emptying most of the board in consecutive moves, leaving behind identical pieces, so close had their thoughts come in reading and countering one another. King, queen, and elephant for each, with five pawns of his against four pawns of hers. A piece less, and yet in spite of the slight disadvantage she won. The queen and elephant combination finished it for her, locking the opponent king behind his own sentinels, while his queen and elephant first watched helplessly from their respective cells, and then in a last futile attempt to save the situation were slain in succession. Her penultimate move was a masterpiece of strategy, offering him seven different ways of choosing defeat.

The king knew that she had won long before, only he had failed to see. He had been completely unsuspicious of any danger when he had removed one of her pawns left dangling in the centre, while she had simply offered it to lure him into a trap. But he was not in the least dispirited, for he had learnt certain lessons in offence that he would have occasion to apply not in play alone but in life too.

Suddenly conscious of the time spent over the board these past two days, he expressed his feelings to the queen. But it was I who wanted to play with you, she offered. Her words had a ring of finality, as if she was making her peace not only with herself, but with history. Perhaps she had already intuited that the game was bound to fall into obscurity sooner than later, and just as this time she had conceived it on the thrust of her own special impulses, other creators, as yet unborn, waited in the wings to do so for other times and ages. For this was the one law from which there was no deviation. Making and unmaking forever and ever with subtle variations was how the web of enchantment was woven.

Later, in bed, lying on his back, she astride him, her legs unusually firm round his waist, digging deep into his flesh, the chin rising away from him, sashing her neck and face in blue shadows, their outlines somewhat diffused and magnified, he felt her to be not herself but a being from beyond come to join with him, work him inside her till the pillar of flesh he was began to heat and burn scarlet, smouldering and disintegrating to ash in the cavernous dark.

XVIII

WEARIED AND ravaged by endless fighting, the two armies girded themselves one more time for the day's ghastly work. Tin-helmeted, smeared in wood smoke and sandalwood lotions, the soldiers rolled on the balls of their feet, gripping their weapons tautily, restless for the impending command to action. We knew the fight was now to the very end, easily forgetting that wars were never truly concluded but only abandoned. Be that as it may, the engagement had entered its final phase, the abandonment near, for lately the demon king, too, had joined the conflict, and was slowly making his way to its epicentre, where the two princes fought with a murderous fervour each day.

Because he moved deep inside this horrid crush unable to observe it from above, the war's unusual pattern, its devilish design, was not easy to discern from the start. For days he did not stop to think whether his movement across the field was as random as it appeared. On nights in the camp, before the dwindling fire, in the period of rest and silence pinched from the violent din of battle, faint beginnings of a pattern sometimes would rise above the impressions wrestling in the arc of his skull, but he could not dwell on it for long, unable as he was to connect it with anything he had known or seen.

Seen though he had, if not grasped clearly, and it would take him years to form the conviction that his fate had for a while come to resemble one of those ivory men he had glimpsed being pushed about on the square board between that man and woman on the night of his mission in the demon king's palace so long ago. Was it the king himself who had been directing from above his movements and those of countless others beside him? Was it ever possible to project the schemes of a board game onto a real war, onto reality itself? And who took his place when he took his place amidst the troops at last? Why had he not seen in the intervening centuries that peculiar game again?

Then, too, the war was *sui generis*, for its cause was not expansion or tribute, not safeguarding the lives of your people or quelling a rebellion that threatened your sovereignty, but something infinitely more complex and obscure. Defending honour, we believed. Perhaps. At least, the answer was easy for us. But what was the king defending, what did he fight for?

Pride, infamy, sinful corruption. These words had been scooped hollow by time's insistent digging, questions that kept mounting in its wake, befuddlement that knew no end. He and he alone could have answered. Ravana, the sage-king. Ravana, the possessed. And maybe not even he. And where was he now, ages away from the day when Rama's arrow had at last made its target, piercing his navel in the softening glow of the declining sun by the beach? He had fallen like any other in battle, immortal until the arrow struck home, dying like everyone else in the end from and of his beliefs.

Been here too long, seen too much, hope ebbing away into emptiness and unease. Now it was melancholy, and now melancholy diffusing into space, and now nothing. The snow peaks had sunk behind the clouds, and here mist was rising from the roots of the trees. Forever and ever, there had always been war, and the promise of peace, of untold everlasting happiness, of rivers that flowed with milk, had that golden age ever been? Or was it just a fancy, a nostalgia, the mind's instinctive bid to escape from its cruel unending predicament, the world in which one found oneself, the world where one always arrived late, with little recourse but to go down fighting against all the odds that continued to rise from day to day? Real or not, the high noon of humanity lay most certainly in the

XVIII

deepest past, now irrecoverable, and the path ahead went steeply down, right to the abyss, and then beyond.

Suddenly the child thought of something, and the dark, brooding feeling was gone. His fingers began to itch. To touch, to grasp, to move. Without a warning he slipped off the tree's crown and came swishing down to the ground, the low branches breaking his fall and landing him straight on his feet. Back in his old form, the god turned to look up the tree and found the puma, already halfway down, following in his wake.

XIX

THE LAST OF the logs had long since crumbled to ash in the braziers, and outside the sky lay awash in a coral-pink luminescence. A faint sweet scent still circled the half-cold cinders, and I felt something akin to happiness rush through me. Or was it relief? Relief at what? At returning alive from the very brink of death?

This crumbling pavilion, together with its three old caretakers who unobtrusively saw to my every need, who were hardly there otherwise, seemed my one true attainment, and to be here and alive, fixed in body and spirit, was reward enough. This when I had least expected or worked for it, even if I had worked for and desired other things.

After a certain point in a man's life, he settles so comfortably into the shell of his aims or, for it is the same thing, the aims work themselves so finely into his skin, that he grows equally remote from both loss and gain, and it is only the distance he has travelled, only how far he has come in his pursuits, that holds any interest, that makes him turn time and again to reckon his vanished steps, but this too without any strong emotion, so that it is sometimes revealed to him that it is in fact the journey which leads to things and not a desire for things that begets the journey.

But maybe it was this and this alone I had wanted from the beginning, and life or fate or time or the jumble of infinite deeds, whatever it was, had seen to my wish while squaring its ledger. You could only end alone when you began so in the first place. This was but fair, just as it was fair that those who arrived together one day

returned together. Misa had followed the king into my world, or
what I imagined to be my world, and so too she chose her exit, if by
a different door, slipping away while I was in the throes of battle,
fighting desperately for the king and for my own life.

Near the evening of what turned out to be the final day of the
war, I was locked in a fierce combat with an enemy soldier who had
quite bravely taken control of one of our elephants. The strain and
wounds of the past months had taken their toll, and I knew I would
not survive for long. And then the accursed or the blessed arrow,
depending on which side you fought, lodged itself in the king's
trunk, and before you knew the weapon had fallen from your hand,
the conflict abruptly abandoned. Thus it occurred to you that not
even of your own story were you the hero. Privilege and history
overran you there as well. Like a pawn clashing in a corner you
watched the game end, your life pardoned, simply because it was
not you who were its focal point, but another someone more
powerful, one on whom things ultimately hinged. Your blood, your
pain, your cruelty were a waste, even if the stain of loss, of disgrace,
would stick to you for as long as you lived.

Yet now this was history, dead, forgotten. A vast river of sleep
flowed between the past and me. And today was different, full of
wellbeing, a fresh beginning. I clutched at this fiction with every bit
of my will. And it grew, this thought, that I had somehow escaped
from history, was outside it, watching it unroll in a procession of
shadowy forms on a cloth-screen in the distance.

Late that day, I went out into the hills. Light lashing through
trees, birds twittering and cooing, busily content in their tiny bird
lives. Some way up, to my left, there was a group of ancient rock-
caves, hidden from view by wild brambles and azalea shrubs, that I
had explored on an earlier outing. The walls inside, wherever light
touched them, were covered in strange dancing figures and
drawings in red, blue, and yellow pigments. I thought of them as I
passed the brush on my way along the hill. Were these childish
sketches or high art from an earlier time? Who could tell? What the

images had meant to those who painted them could now not be discerned, was lost forever. Time was always mocking us, deluding us, here bestowing grandeur on our follies, and there turning our artistry to childish doodles.

Webbed in such thoughts, I emerged from the trees at the head of the knoll. There again was the ancient bell hanging from its rotting wooden structure, between one aeon and another, the sole visible peg in the fabric of time. I hadn't noticed that the sun had gone behind a bank of cloud, while several others were rushing to cover the sky from end to end. Soon only to the north a patch of blue remained, the eye of heaven that was fast closing, withdrawing from us, locking our age and our misdeeds in the trap of our own making, snuffing out here and now the prevailing stench of our bloody history. Was I then the last witness breathing in the last of my time's air, which, regardless of the reek of history, came to me laden with the scent of ancient trees?

This age must end, I thought, drifting toward the bell, for a new age to dawn. An age that would revere not the grand, the awe-full, the terrifying, but the small, the commonplace, the briefness of gesture. And, because of this simple turn of attention, rise in triumph over all others. An age of poets, an age for poets.

I moved my fingers over the rough, slowly corroding surface of the bell and, drawing all my strength into my arms, struck the heavy gong with both hands, marking at once the closure of the old and the coming of the new.

For their generous advice and support, I am deeply grateful to David Brooks, J.M. Coetzee, Michael Hulse, Satend Nandan, and Vanessa Smith.

At Roundfire we publish great stories. We lean towards the spiritual and thought-provoking. But whether it's literary or popular, a gentle tale or a pulsating thriller, the connecting theme in all Roundfire fiction titles is that once you pick them up you won't want to put them down.